Z Chronicles: Surge of the Dead

By A.L.White

To my Uncle John, who has always supported me and taught me to be the person that I am today

Virginia and Lori have survived the first wave of the Zombie Apocalypse by relying on wit and skills imparted by the harsh realities of their new world and the guidance of their companions. Enduring a world where all they knew and loved has perished has taken quite a toll on the girls but they soldier on regardless; ever determined to continue their journey on old Bob's map.

This is the second book in the Z Chronicles, a series of adventures crafted as my imagination runs wild. If thirst for a new perspective on zombie stories then come into my world for a story or two.

When the Lamb broke the fourth seal, I heard the voice of the fourth living creature saying, "Come." I looked, and behold, an ashen horse; and he who sat on it had the name Death; and Hades was following with him. Authority was given to them over a fourth of the earth, to kill with sword and with famine and with pestilence and by the wild beasts of the earth.

Revelation 6:7-8

CHAPTER 1

Virginia sat outside in the cold, chilling air watching Lori and Jonas drive away in the truck. If anyone should have been in that truck, it was her and she did not understand why he could not see that. In the past few months no one had become as good as she had at hunting and killing zombies. It was like second nature now; easier with each passing day. Even the two point zeroes were nothing to Virginia. Rarely did she mention that; Bob had told her to try to steer clear of them because they were smarter than the normal ones.

The door opened behind her and Jack came through, he nodded his head, and went over by the trailer. That was where he spent the better part of his day; with the laptop plugged into the solar panels. Virginia wanted to tell him, at least a million times, that it was all a waste of his time. If he was so smart and could not figure out the simplest thing as that, then maybe he was not as bright as everyone had thought. They were all as good as dead. The sooner he

1

learned that, the better off he would be; maybe he would even stop being dead weight in her mind. Still, she did like Jack, in his own way he was a loner like her. Even before the world moved on, Virginia did not have many friends. The ones she did have more or less tolerated her, she thought. Funny, she could not remember how many times they had called her a crybaby growing up. They would all be surprised now to see that she had no more tears left to cry. Why would she? Even if she felt like she wanted to, who would care? What would it change? All of her family, with the exception of Lori, were dead and it probably would not be too long before she was. Lori kept talking about things that did not matter anymore. Virginia did not see a point in remembering. It was too hard to face, and served no purpose in the world that they lived in now. Mom was not coming home with dinner. Dad could not look over the arrows she made yesterday and say, "good job pumpkin." They were gone and that is where she wanted to leave them. No pleasant thoughts of family time to clutter up her mind when she had to concentrate. If anyone here was useful to Virginia, it was Bob. She and he had hit it off right away.

Bob was a little bit like her dad but more real somehow. Dad had pretended to be prepping for the end of the world; Bob did prepare for the end of the world.

The door opened behind her, causing Virginia to lose her train of thought. She turned around to see Bob coming slowly towards her. He sat down off to her left where Zeus and Perseus joined him on either side. Virginia pretended not to see him, still upset over his objections to her going into town at breakfast.

"So that's how it's going to be?" he asked her.

Virginia rolled her eyes but did not answer.

"I guess you could have gone into town with your sister. Of course, then me and the lads would have had to do this other job," he stated.

Virginia let out a sigh, she could tell when Bob was trying to play her, and this was one of those times if she had ever seen one.

"The lads and I are going to go out and reconnoiter the area," he said to the back

3

of her head. "You know what reconnoiter is?"

Virginia laughed a low shallow laugh, "To go scout an area?"

Bob put his hand on her shoulder to get Virginia's full attention. "Yes, that is what it is, young lady. We need to know that our area is safe to stay in for the time being, if we are going to stay here for the winter, that is."

"Safe? We haven't seen a person, dead or alive, other than the people in this group!"

"The other night Zeus there was acting a little odd. I think something may be out there and we need someone to look. I could send the lads, but they can't talk. I guess I can take them for a walk to have a look see, might do me and them some good to stretch our legs."

Virginia was not stupid by any means and she knew that if she did not go, Bob would definitely go. He would go just because, now that he had asked her, she was refusing. He knew that his heart was not holding out as well as they had hoped. He was growing weaker every day and everyone knew it. No one said anything aloud for whatever reason.

"I will take the pups and have a look around if it will stop you from nagging all day long," Virginia finally said, managing to smile at him.

One of the few things that made Virginia still feel human was when Bob smiled at her as he was doing now. It was the way her father used to smile at her when she did something right. "Where do you think I should start?"

Bob thought a minute and then said, "Start over that way, towards the farm we passed coming in here. The lads seem to sniff the air in that direction a lot lately."

She knew exactly where Bob was talking about, and he knew that she had been there a few times while she was hunting. There was not much there besides the old farmhouse and the barn, but she would go look and make Bob happy. Besides, it would give her something to do other than her chores.

"Let me grab a few things, and the Lads and I will go scout it out," she stated, climbing to her feet.

"Virginia," Bob said halting her, "you run into anything out there, you get safe little lady. If you have to, climb as high as you can and wait it out. Never mind the lads, they will take care of themselves, you hear?"

Virginia paused for a moment and continued on, returning with a backpack and more arrows.

"Come on boys, let's go," she said to the lads.

As she headed with the dogs toward the gate Bob called out her name, but she kept going. He called out again, "Virginia!"

"I will get high if I run into anything Bob, promise." She said as they neared the gate.

Opening the gate, she let the dogs go through first and then followed. Perseus ran forward about twenty feet and then dove into the snowy undergrowth of the ditch. Virginia and Zeus ran as fast as they could to see what he had found. Only to find it was the puppy in Perseus coming out again. She laughed at him and called for him to come on. The whole way towards the farm Zeus walked to her right-side keeping pace while Perseus would bolt up a head then return trying to get on her right side. A playful snap from Zeus sent him off charging ahead again.

Virginia loved being out here by herself with the dogs. Here in their company she felt free of any worries. She took care of them and they took care of her.

Reaching the beginning of the long gravel driveway leading to the farmhouse, Virginia stopped, looking around and listening for any movement that seemed unnatural. A swing hanging from an old tree about ten feet in front of the front porch swung gently in the wind. A broken shutter, hanging by a single fastener, banged against the windowsill. Satisfied that there were no other movements or sounds that stuck out to her, Virginia moved forward. Zeus took the lead with Perseus staying a few feet to her left. He was not running off to play now. Virginia thought it was amazing how he knew it was time to be serious. Slowly they made their way past the swing and up the crumbling sidewalk to the porch stairs. Virginia started to step up but halted as Zeus turned sideways in front of her. She could see that the door was ajar and knew what he wanted.

"Well then, go ahead and check it out. What are you waiting for?"

Zeus went up the stairs with Perseus and nudged the door open. After standing there for a few minutes sniffing they disappeared into the building. Virginia looked around as she stood there impatiently, waiting for the all clear. The wait was not long as Perseus came running out of the house with a tennis ball in his mouth. At the top of the porch, Zeus's big head popped into the door opening and she knew all was clear inside.

"It's about time," she said, laughing at him as she climbed the old stairway onto the porch. Zeus backed up a few steps to let her and Perseus into the house. The room had an old brown, full size sofa and a love seat arranged in an L shape towards the outside walls. Next to the door, going into the next room, was a rocking chair. Just like the ones Virginia had seen outside of a restaurant that her father loved going to for breakfast when she was small. The walls were covered with pictures of what she had assumed where the previous owners and their family. In the next room, she found the kitchen, like the previous room it was clean, but looked well worn and old. Out of reflex, Virginia opened the refrigerator door, letting

out a horrid smell that even backed up the
dogs. Slamming the door closed, she froze
and listened for any movement. She was
mad because it was a careless move to
make. Something she knew better than to
do.

At the back of the kitchen she found
a stairway leading to the second floor. It too
looked old and narrow. Not enough room for
her and one of the dogs to go up next to side
by side and it seemed hard for Zeus to
climb. Once up there it was more of the
same, the furniture was old and falling apart.
It looked like the family had left. Maybe the
authorities had taken them. Either way,
Virginia was satisfied that the house was
empty and safe. She returned downstairs and
started out the kitchen door to the head
towards the barn. Zeus and Perseus nearly
knocked her off her feet passing her by just
as she began to step. Perseus had the tennis
ball again as if to say, "Ok we are safe, let's
play." Virginia called him over to her, took
the ball from him, and threw it as far as she
could. Perseus charged off to retrieve the
ball while Zeus sat down and crooked his
head, watching. When Perseus returned,
Virginia held the ball in front of Zeus and
said, "Come on old guy, let's play a little."
She smiled as she threw the ball nearly to

the barn. A laugh escaped her when Zeus knocked Perseus over trying to get an unfair advantage in the race for the ball.

It was in that moment that she had appeared; from out of the depths of Virginia's soul, a place hidden deep from the world and safe. It was the real Virginia. From the times before her mom had gotten sick, before her dad had been dragged from the house by the emergency services people, and long before her brother had died so violently. There in the field between the house and barn she was running around and laughing like a kid again. Every now and then a scream would escape her, as she wrestled the ball away from the dogs and threw it again. She was having such a good time that she had lost track of time and everything else around her. Only when it looked like Zeus had laid down refusing to chase the ball did she take notice of the movement around them circling in closer. Zeus did not growl or move; he just laid there panting as if he could not catch his breath. Perseus moved in front of both of them and growled.

Virginia reached for her crossbow, but it was gone. She had laid it down on the ground about thirty feet away from her. Her head snapped from the bow to the zombies.

They were closer, by far, but slower. In a mad dash, she ran towards the bow; a shadow came from her left closing within inches. It quickly went down as Perseus attacked the creature, knocking it off its feet, and to the ground.

Virginia put an arrow into the crossbow and spun towards Perseus, busy tearing the throat out of the zombie. She called him to her side and backed towards Zeus who was still lying on his side panting. There were too many for her to fight. Even more, Virginia thought, than there had been outside of the lab where they patched up Bob and Jack.

When she reached Zeus, she yelled at him to get up and move. Zeus lifted his head up and stared at her with pleading eyes. It looked to Virginia like he was hurt and afraid for the first time since she had met the dogs at Bob's house. Then, from where he was laying, Zeus saw the zombies cross into his field of vision. Something inside him willed him to his feet, driving him to protect Virginia. Once up and moving forward, slowly, on unsteady legs, he pulled his lips back into a snarl bearing his massive teeth. Virginia patted him on the head and moved backwards towards the barn. It was the only path left to them, and it seemed the safest right now.

With each step backward the herd surged forward. Slowly, like a train on a track, toward them. Perseus stayed right by Virginia's side with Zeus still blocking the path between her and the approaching zombies.

A hand reached from the side, grabbing a hold of Zeus, and he turned into it snapping his maw like crazy. Virginia shot an arrow into the head of one zombie as Zeus vanished from sight. As she reached the barn door Virginia could still hear him growling and fighting the herd off. Perseus moaned for his companion and right then, Zeus broke free of the herd, running to his companions. Virginia swung the door open enough for them to get through and slammed it closed behind her. On the door, there was a clumsy looking lock that she latched and then pulled an old box over in front of it.

Surprisingly, the barn was fairly well lit by the light streaming through the random holes in the loft rafters. Virginia could hear the sounds of the herd moving around the barn as they enveloped it. The door was probably the weakest point, she thought, and even that opened outward. The makeshift latch should hold unless they had grown smarter and knew to pull it outward. Zeus seemed to be doing a little better as he lay down on the hard dirt floor in front of her. She would check on him as soon as the rest of the barn had been checked out. In the back, just on the other side of a green tractor it looked like there was a stair case off to the right, in the shadows.

Raising her crossbow, Virginia moved toward it. When she noticed Perseus moving to her side she told him to stay. If anything did pop out, Zeus would need all the help he could get right now. On she went, towards the shadows, to see if that was what she had thought it was. It would make her a whole lot happier to stay up off the ground floor if she could. The murmur of the zombies outside made it harder to concentrate on the job at hand. Her eyes were looking forward trying to make out every shape, but her mind and ears were wandering towards the noise.

Just beyond the large tire on the tractor, Virginia could finally make out the stairs and a barrel of some sort. The stairs looked better than the stairs inside of the house. They creaked with every step she took. Funny how so much noise could surround her but her senses could hone in on one single thing; so much so that the sounds it created were as loud as a gun going off. With each step she was growing more tense and ready to spring on something, anything; the anxiety building until she reached the top step.

For the most part, the loft was empty. A few bales of hay, but that was it. On the far end, above the door they had come in through, there was another large door. Virginia walked over to it and swung it open so that she could see. There before her were thousands of zombies. There were still quite a few in front of the barn and moving around the house, but the rest of the herd was moving off towards the road.

Returning to the dogs, Virginia petted Zeus on the head for a few minutes. Reassuring them both with the motion. Perseus, feeling like he was being slighted, pushed his head under her hand.

"OK, you too; let's go upstairs and get some rest while they clear out of here." She said as she helped Zeus get up and led them to the stairs. Perseus went up without a problem but the older Zeus needed help up the stairs. It had crossed her mind, briefly halfway up, that maybe it would have been better to just leave him down stairs. The thought didn't last long because she was closer to these two dogs than anyone alive. If he had stayed downstairs, they all would have had to stay downstairs.

Once at the top Zeus seemed to have caught his second wind and he followed Virginia on his own without help. They all settled down in front of the open door and watched the herd move away from the area. Zeus laid his head in Virginia's lap and went to sleep. Perseus lay down on the other side, looking out the door too. It wasn't too long before he and Virginia had joined Zeus in a deep sleep as their bodies tried to recover after the afternoon's excitement. It was the first sound sleep that Virginia could remember having since her mom grew sick and was taken away.

The rest only lasted for a little while even though to Virginia it felt as though it could have been hours. The gun shots rang through the silent air, echoing off the barn walls. Then the horrible screams reached her. Immediately she knew that someone at the bunker had been caught by the herd, maybe everyone. Jumping to her feet, startling the dogs, Virginia started to head down the stairs and then it was silent again. Moving back to the loft door she listened as hard as she could for any signs of life. Just a single sound of a voice was all she wanted, or a gun shot. Nothing came. It was then that the realization that she was truly alone came washing over her. In her mind she went over and over how this could have happened. Then it struck her, like being hit in the face with a brick. In the morning, when they had left, Perseus was running around playing. She had run up to where he was to see what he had found, leaving the gate wide open. No one at the bunker would have stood a chance if they were not keeping watch. The only ones who seemed to ever keep watch was her, Lori, Jonas and the dogs. With them all gone she knew that Jack probably never raised his nose from the laptop. Even if he had looked up, once his mind went to work he barely noticed anything else around him.

Reaching out in front of her she pulled the large door to her and heard it latch. There was no way of knowing if anyone survived at the bunker for now. The herd would need to move on just as it had moved into the area before she or the dogs could try to get back there. She wondered if Lori had made it back ok. There was no way of knowing if they had driven past her while she was playing with the dogs. Sometime

later, overwhelmed and uncertain, Virginia
fell into a deep sleep.

****

Some folks called it the unofficial
neighborhood association, others called it
the Briar subdivision men's gossip session.
It didn't really matter what it was called
because it happened every Saturday around
nine am until it was too cold for anyone to
take sitting on Doc Stewarts' patio. There
were a few that even kept it up once winter
had firmly set in by moving inside to Doc's
kitchen table. Charlie Harris was one of the
die-hards that rarely, if ever, missed it.

Charlie Harris was born and raised
right in Rivers Crossing. Most of his
younger years were spent dreaming about
living anywhere but there. The plan had
always been to attend one of the state
universities, and then, move as far away as
he could. Sometime in High School that plan
began to fade. When his father took ill,
Charlie went to work full time in the family-
owned diner. His grades suffered and the
university dream died a little more with each
table he'd clean. Sometime in the fall of
ninety-nine, with medical bills adding up

and business steadily declining, his father closed the diner and declared bankruptcy. It wasn't very long after that when his dad passed away.

Charlie worked odd jobs on local farms to make ends meet for him and his mother. Not wanting her son to turn into another sad story about a young man who stayed in Rivers Crossing living a life of regret, Babe Harrison encouraged her son to move north and find a good job. After a lot of debate back and forth on the subject, Charlie set out for a better job. Loading up his beat up seventy-two Malibu, he set off with a full tank of gas and little else. Settling in Leesville, about an hour and a half away from Rivers Crossing, he found work as a laborer in a small machine shop. The work was hard and the hours were long, but it was a good living. It was there that he met Annie Lincoln, a receptionist. A year later they were married.

In the beginning, Charlie returned home every Sunday to have dinner with his mother. After meeting Annie, that fell to twice a month, then to every other holiday. It just seemed that there was never enough time to make the trip to Rivers Crossing. He worked long hours all week, and Annie was going to school online to get her degree.

Having only Sunday off, Charlie liked to vegetate and watch whatever sporting event was on the television. Annie seemed to have an ever growing amount of homework that she spent the weekend completing.

In two thousand eight Charlie's mother was diagnosed with cancer. She refused to move to where she could get better treatment. Charlie and Annie, at Annie's insistence, moved in with her to help out as much as they could. Luckily, Rivers Crossing was in the beginning of a short lived boom. A canning company had moved into the old bottle plant just outside of town. Main Street saw shuttered buildings like Walt's Diner and the Movie Palace reopened and repurposed. They even had a MacDonald's open up on the grounds where Kermit's filling station had been.

Babe Harris passed away a year after they settled in with her. Charlie inherited the paid off house, so they stayed. They couldn't complain much; Charlie worked at the canning plant for a decent wage, and Annie did web and logo design from home. They were not rich, by any means, but they were happy and decided it was time to start a family. That was when the housing bubble burst and the economy tanked. The canning plant closed, putting Charlie out of work, and Annie found it harder to find freelance design work. The idea of the family was put off until a future date when they both had steady employment.

Charlie tried to talk Annie into moving back to the big city, closer to her family. Annie wouldn't even consider it. She considered Rivers Crossing her home now, and Charlie thought she had settled in too well to the small town way of life. Her argument always ended with the fact that they owned the house outright and the rest of the country didn't seem like they were faring very well either. It seemed too risky to Annie to just pack up and leave. Charlie collected unemployment for as long as it lasted then returned to looking towards the local farms for odd jobs.

It was around that time that Jerimiah "Doc" Stone moved in next door. Doc had retired from a successful private practice in Chicago. He would tell Charlie that he grew up in a small town like Rivers Crossing and had always longed to return to the simpler way of life. What started out as a few short talks at their property lines quickly morphed into Saturday morning Coffee. Before they knew it more of the neighborhood early birds were joining in and it officially moved to Doc's patio. Charlie liked it over there because unlike his yard, Doc worked hard at creating his version of an English garden. Called it his 'little slice of heaven on Earth,' and Charlie tended to agree with him.

This morning when he arrived, the usual crowd was missing and only Pete Wilson was there. Pete lived on the other side of Doc and had the distinction of being one of the few people that could get a rise out of Doc on occasion.

Pete nodded his head as he sat down and Doc handed over a fresh cup of coffee. In the background the Bixby local a.m. news station was playing.

"There! Did you hear that?" Pete was asking Doc, "The mainstream media has jumped on board with this whole pandemic story."

"I hardly think a small a.m. station in Bixby counts as main stream media, Peter!"

"Why wouldn't it? They could easily be owned by some media conglomerate and that is what they want us common folk to think!"

Doc shook his head no, almost violently, "If that was true Peter, how would you explain the simple fact that Rivers Crossing has so many cases of it?"

"Cases of what?" Charlie asked, causing Pete to spit out his coffee and Doc to sigh loudly.

Pete then gave Charlie a disappointing look and said, "Charlie do you even watch the news or pay any attention to what we talk about on Sundays?"

Had he not felt as if he had been rebuked he would have laughed at that. In fact, he rarely paid attention to most of their conversations. Mostly they were Pete ranting about the liberals trying to take everything he had worked hard for away from him. Following that was Doc stating that no one wanted what Pete had.

"Charlie, there has been a national curfew put into place because of the flu outbreak." Doc stated, as if he were talking to a young kid, "They say this one could be a life altering event it is so bad."

"Annie doesn't like watching the news much, says it is all just too depressing for her."

"How do you find out what the weather is going to be like?" Pete asked.

Charlie smiled at him, "Either I hear it here from you two, or I just see what it is like when I walk out the door. If it is raining, it's raining. If it is sunny, it's sunny." Letting that sink in, he continued, "Besides, if there is a national curfew then what are we doing here now?"

"Who in the hell are you expecting to enforce it in Rivers Crossing?" Pete asked. "Sheriff

Hernandez? We have known Joel since we were all kids; even he will tell you that he is more of a glorified security guard than he is law enforcement. Whatever happens in Rivers Crossing? Nothing!"

"Is it really that bad Doc?" Charlie asked.

Doc looked up at the clouds for a minute like he was searching for an answer then said, "Charlie, this is a bug like none I have ever seen. It strikes fast, and kills even faster. Hospitals in Bixby and Long Tree are at full capacity from what I hear. I can't even get a straight answer from my old friends in Chicago as to what it is."

The phone rang twice and Doc's wife, Bess, came to the sliding glass door and motioned for him. "Will you guys excuse me for a minute while I see what this is about?" Doc asked.

"I have to run, Doc," Pete said as he climbed out of the chair and nodded his head at Charlie. A few minutes later Doc returned and asked if they could shut this week short and make up for it next week.

"What's wrong Doc?" Charlie asked.

"The mayor wants to set up a make shift hospital of sorts in town," Doc replied.

"Where? There is no place that could be used for a hospital."

"I believe they are deciding between using the new school or the behemoth next to the church," Doc replied.

Charlie laughed at that. The behemoth was what the town's people called the 'old school' that was built during the Great Depression. The actual name of the school was the Franklin Delano Roosevelt School. It was far too large for Rivers Crossings' needs from the moment the design was presented. Most people figured it was a way to put people to work from the surrounding area. As far as Charlie knew, he was one of the last classes to go there, and that was second or third grade. It was decided that for so few students the cost didn't justify using the old building anymore. "I think they would be better off with the new school," Charlie replied.

"I agree. That is exactly what I told the Mayor last night," Doc said, "I guess Bess and I will find out which building it is in about an hour or so. We're going down to help set up a triage area."

"You need any help Doc; you know where I am at."

"I know Charlie. For right now I think it's best for you and Annie to stay inside. No reason to take chances," Doc stated.

Charlie shook his head that he understood what Doc was saying. "Speaking of Annie, I should be getting back home about now."

When he got home Annie was sleeping on the couch with one of her true crime dramas playing on the television. Charlie walked over to get a closer look at her and noticed how puffy her face seemed to be. *Her allergies seem to be getting the best of her this time*, Charlie thought to himself. Then he noticed how unbelievably hot the house was. Annie was not above cranking up the heat when she wasn't feeling well and this was one of those times. Charlie quickly decided that it would be best just to let her sleep so that he could get a few things done around the house. They generally shared all the work around the house so doing a little extra, while Annie battled what he hoped was the last of the allergy problems, didn't bother him at all. Besides, not having a job to go to had taught Charlie to find busy work around the house just to keep his sanity. If he ever let any sign of depression show it would hit Annie twice as hard. She had always had issues with depression. Teetering on a thin line between being deeply depressed and as she called it, 'feeling good.' It never made a difference to him, he prayed for her to feel good, but loved her just as much when she was depressed. Sometimes they would go for walks along the river just taking in the scenery. It cheered Annie up and that was all that mattered to Charlie.

Looking around the house he decided that he would do the laundry. On more than one occasion Annie had tried to teach him to do it the way she liked. Charlie just couldn't make sense of most of her method in his own mind. That made it harder to do it that way, so he didn't. Deep down, the whole hot water, cold water part was a bunch of hoo-ha. All that mattered to Charlie was that there was soap in the machine. He chuckled as he loaded the wash machine; Annie would have a fit if she saw how full it was. *Oh well*, Charlie thought, *she is asleep and what she don't know will not hurt her--or get him in trouble.*

Later on Charlie cooked them soup and grilled cheese sandwiches for dinner. That was what he preferred when he did not feel well growing up, and he figured you never know what could possibly help.

Annie ate a little of the soup and a few bites of grilled cheese. Soon after that they lay in bed where Annie fell back asleep while Charlie watched a move.

On Sunday morning when Charlie woke up, Annie wasn't in bed. He looked around and then found her in the family room, sitting in the dark. Charlie was so used to trying to not wake Annie up most mornings that he had grown used to not turning any lights on. Having grown up in the house, he knew it like the back of his own hand and lights weren't necessary.

"Charlie, is that you?" Annie asked in a raspy voice.

"Unless you snuck some other guy in that I didn't see," he replied jokingly. "Why are you sitting in the dark honey? Are you ok?"

"Turn the light on," Annie replied.

Charlie reached over to where he knew the light switch was and flipped it first up, and then down, and back up again.

"I promise you, honey, I paid the bill. We are one month behind, but they have never turned it off as long as I paid the past due amount," Charlie pleaded his case.

Annie's voice softened a little but was still raspy, "I know you did, Charlie. I think the whole neighborhood is out."

Charlie went to the front room window and looked out at the pitch black street. Looking first towards the right he noticed no lights on at any of the houses. To the left brought more of the same, just black.

As he walked back into the family room, Charlie became aware of how chilly the house had become. "Honey, would you like me to see how much firewood we have left? Maybe there is enough to make a fire."

"Could you, baby? It is so cold in here," Annie replied.

Charlie went into the kitchen and dragged a chair over to the refrigerator. He was a decent height at five feet-nine inches, but that didn't help when it came to getting the emergency candles and flashlight from the cupboard above the fridge.

"Damn." He stated under his breath as he felt something fall from the top of the fridge. He had a good idea that it was the basket Annie had used to put fake colored Easter eggs in last Easter. The one he had promised to put up since, well, since Easter ended. The cupboard door opened and he began to feel around for the candles or the flashlight. The first thing he found was a decorative candle in a jar. Bringing that out, he climbed down and felt around for his smokes on the counter. Finding the half empty pack he also found the lighter he was looking for. In an instant they were no longer sitting in the dark. Charlie placed the candle on the cut-through between the kitchen and the family room.

"Things are looking brighter all ready," Annie joked.

"Well if you like that you're going to love this," Charlie joked back as he pulled the flashlight out and pointed it at her. With the flick of the switch Annie was bathed in

29

light. Charlie paused for a minute thinking just how beautiful his wife was, even with her allergies at their worst.

Climbing down, Charlie headed towards the back door, "Ok, now for some firewood," he stated as he went outside.

The night was still with a cold north wind blowing. Charlie had never seen a night this dark in his whole life. It made him feel like Annie and he were the last people left on Earth and it scared him a little. There wasn't a lot of firewood left to burn because they had put off buying a face cord for this year. Annie said there really wasn't money in the budget with the way their job situations had left them. Charlie was sorry now that he had listened to her. He grabbed as many of the logs as he could while holding the flashlight and returned to the house.

Charlie lit a nice sized fire then headed out to the garage to find his camping supplies. He would bring in the coffee pot that they used over an open fire and the sleeping bags. That should hold them until the power came back on.

****

CHAPTER 2

After Virginia left, Bob went back into the bunker to rest a little. These days he found himself feeling worn out more often than not. Little catnaps seem to help most days; enough for him to get by. Other days he felt like, if not for a little knowledge on survival and forethought to prepare for the unseen calamity, he would have been useless to the group. Sitting in his favorite chair, Bob could feel the vice tightening around his chest again. Bob reached for the meds that Julie had given him. A glass of water would have been nice, but the lecture he would have gotten with it wouldn't be. Looking toward the kitchen he could see Julie in there reorganizing something. She did that a lot, and Bob knew, for her, it was a way of coping with the situation. The good thing about this group he knew was that each had found a way to deal with the end of life as they knew it. Everyone with the exception of Virginia; she had shut the past out completely. For now that was her strength to get through each day. Bob felt himself nodding off into a deep slumber.

In his dream Bob was back in his back yard with the lads. There wasn't a cloud in the sky and a slight breeze from the west was making the eighty-five-degree day bearable. Perseus was doing his best to get Zeus to play with him. Zeus, at eleven years old, was more content to sit in the shade provided by the table's umbrella while he waited for Bob to drop something from the grill. Bob reached down and patted his old friend's head and Zeus responded by licking his hand.

"You have always been here for me, haven't you, old friend?" Bob said to Zeus as Perseus nudged his head in between Bob's hand and Zeus's head. "We can't forget our oversized puppy can we?" Bob said as he brought his other hand over to push Perseus off of Zeus and then scratched the side of his head just below the ear.

Bob didn't know what he was cooking on the grill but it smelled great for a moment, but only a moment. Suddenly it smelled putrid, like the meat had rotted while cooking. Then there was a scream that only Bob heard; the lads paid no attention to it at all. The smell wafting from the grill was so rancid Bob could barely take it; then, another scream.

32

Bob would never know what exactly woke him up. It could have been the stench, or it could have been the scream. The last thing he saw was a grotesquely deteriorated head with maggots spilling out of the scalp as it closed its mouth over his neck.

****

By Thursday it had become apparent the power wasn't going to come back on and Charlie was starting to worry. Even more clear was that Annie wasn't having her normal allergy issues. Sometime during the night her fever had dropped, which Charlie took as a good sign. This morning however her body temperature didn't even register on the bargain-priced electronic thermometer they owned. In the sunlight her beautiful pale skin looked grayish in hue with veins in her arm and face prominently showing. Charlie threw the last of the logs on the fire when a knock came at the front door. He walked in a half daze filled with worry over Annie, to the door, and opened it.

"Charlie! I was wondering how you and Annie were doing," Doc's forced yet still pleasant smile greeted him.

"Come on in, Doc. Do you think you could have a look at Annie while you're here?" Charlie asked.

Doc shook his head yes and followed Charlie into the family room. It only took one look from across the room and Doc knew what it was and where it was heading quickly.

"How long has she been like this?" Doc asked as he moved closer to Annie.

Charlie shook his head slowly because he still couldn't believe the change over night. "She looked like that this morning, when I woke up."

Doc backed across the room and took Charlie by the arm, "Charlie, you need to come with me and see something now, while there is still time."

"I don't think I should leave her right now, Doc. She may wake up and wonder where I am off to."

"Charlie, do me just this one favor and come for a ride with me, ok? I promise you Annie will be lying right where she is when you get back."

Reluctantly Charlie agreed to go for the ride as long as it would be a short one.

Doc led him out to the car and motioned him to get in. They drove downtown on deserted streets, past deserted shops until they pulled into the small Sheriff substation. Doc parked in the parking lot and again motioned for Charlie to follow him without saying a word as to why.

Once inside Charlie froze at the sight of Red Harken, slumped over on a desk, drenched in blood. Doc saw what he was looking at, "Red couldn't take it anymore…so he took the easy way out of this mess. Pay no attention to him for now and come with me." Doc then led Charlie back to the small holding cell area, where there were four cells. Charlie had never been back there, but had heard there were four cells in a town that barely ever needed one.

"Ok, Charlie, I am going to open this door. You need to prepare yourself for what you're going to see."

Charlie shook his head ok, still not understanding what was going on and still shocked from the sight of Red. Doc pulled the door open. One of the first things that hit Charlie was the stench of decaying meat. That was followed by the odd breathing sounds, like Annie was making at home. They walked slowly into the holding area and Doc pulled Charlie to the exact center of the aisle.

"Do they look familiar, Charlie?" Doc asked. "These are your friends and neighbors. Pay close attention to the color of their skin, will you? Looks about the same as Annie's doesn't it?"

Charlie started to turn to leave when he noticed a corpse in the back of the first cell. A body that wasn't moving around or discolored like the rest.

"Oh, you seem to have found Deputy Martins. He wouldn't believe what we told him about these folks. He paid for that in a gruesome way; I can tell you. Red went in the other room, and well... you have seen the outcome of that."

Charlie folded over and started vomiting as he unconsciously moved closer to the cell bars. The growling and hissing became deafening as Doc shoved him out of the holding area. Charlie regained his composure and stormed out of the station heading back to his house.

"Charlie! Hold on a minute, will you?" Doc yelled after him.

"Why, Doc? Why did you bring me down here?"

"Because… after I saw Annie, I knew that you would need to see this to believe me," Doc replied.

Charlie stopped and turned on Doc, "Believe what? I don't know what I just saw, or what it has to do with Annie and me!"

"Charlie, just settle down for a minute will you, please? And let's talk," Doc pleaded.

"Why? So you can tell me that my Annie is that!" Charlie shouted, pointing to the station.

"Listen son, the hardest thing I have ever had to do was to give a person and their families what amounted to a death sentence. Bad news like this is never easy to receive, no matter how prepared you are. You can deny it and live what is left of Annie's life, and yours, in denial or you can come to terms with it right now."

Charlie knew deep down that something was wrong with Annie; and it wasn't a little thing. Deep down he didn't know if there was a life after Annie that he wanted to be a part of. Some men say that about their significant others and probably only mean it at face value. Charlie loved Annie with every part of his being. Annie made living through all the bad times worth while. She made getting up in the morning and trying to find a job where there were no jobs to find so much less of a burden than it should have been.

Tears began to trickle down his cheeks and Charlie looked into Doc's eyes looking for a reprieve or a way out. This time his old friend had no such trick up his sleeves. "Would you put Bess in a place like that, Doc?" Charlie asked.

Doc looked down to the ground, "I had to shoot Bess, Charlie. She was one of the first that turned that way. She tore the neck out of a National Guard who was helping in the gym."

The pair stood there, quiet, for a long time, listening to the silence when Charlie spoke up, "Can I lock her up at home, Doc?"

Doc shook his head yes. "Let me drive you back home, Charlie, and I will help you make her as comfortable as we can in a secure room,"

Charlie shook his head yes and started walking back to the car.

CHAPTER 3

Perseus heard it first, responding with an excited moan, and the pounding of his tail against the floor of the loft. Zeus followed suit, dragging Virginia from her slumber.

The unmistakable sound of an engine grinding gears filled the air outside.

Virginia pushed on the latch, causing the door to make a popping sound as it swung open. The truck was swerving all over the road, moving at a slow but steady pace. Watching it near the intersection began to raise Virginia's spirits for a few minutes until the two yellow busses came into view on course to ram the truck. They watched helplessly as the truck barely missed the lead bus, crashing into a stalled car on the far side of the highway. The resulting crash was so loud that Virginia looked all around for the return of the herd, until she was satisfied that there was no sign of them.

****

Before his wife got sick and was taken away along with three of his children, Albert Herman was a faceless voice on an international helpdesk. It wasn't his dream job, by any stretch of the word; in fact, he had pretty much stayed there for the insurance and to have a paycheck. He had worked the early shift which allowed him to spend more time with the younger kids than he had ever spent with his oldest boy, Joe. That was something he figured was the cause of Joe constantly getting into some trouble or another. That was a mistake he wasn't going to make with the other three. Every knee scrape or school function they would see their father was there to lend a helping hand. Not that he thought he was completely to blame for Joe's actions; just that he was hedging his bet with the others. Life wasn't perfect, they didn't have a lot of extra money to do the things his coworkers did, or take long expensive trips to exotic locations. He had lost his job to outsourcing back in two thousand ten, right after the wife's company closed its doors for good; but they had survived.

It was a Sunday afternoon when the local emergency management group had shown up on his doorstep. The euphoric feeling of being saved passed when the men explained that they had an order to remove anyone with the infection for the good of those that where healthy in the area. That was Albert's first clue that all wasn't right in the world. Looking back now, there were so many signs that were just overlooked. Maybe he wanted to see the world like it was or had been. That was a mistake that Al promised himself he would never make again. They took his wife and small children outside, toward a large, gray prison bus, or at least what Al thought looked like a prison bus. It could have been military; he didn't know for sure. What he did know was that a man wearing a gas mask came out of the bus, stopping his wife and children from getting on. Four shots to the head later, they were no more. That was what he saw every night when he tried to sleep. It haunted him during the hours he was awake sometimes; always there just under the surface waiting to erupt. After that Joe didn't talk to him and the two lived in the house, barricaded away from the world. Time stopped in Al's mind so he couldn't remember how long it had been that they stayed that way. Food was running out, the power had gone off, and there wasn't a lot of water. Joe would sometimes mutter things under his breath, then sneer at him, but that was it. One day there was a knock on the door again. They both turned three shades of pale as they looked into each other's eyes. There was no mistaking the fear that petrified them until a familiar voice called out; a voice that Al knew well and thought he would never hear again. They both raced to the door, throwing it open, to find old Aunt Zoe standing there smiling at them. That was how they ended up there on the road, in two school busses that they stole from the local school yard. Aunt Zoe had informed Al and Joe that it was their Christian duty to find others who had survived and take them to a place she had heard about on the emergency radio at the retirement home. The buses would be needed so that they wouldn't have to turn anyone away, she had said. So far that wasn't much of a problem; they rescued three children. There were not many living people to be found. If there were, they were hidden well, and Al was not about to go on a door to door search in every town they drove through. Even though, he figured, if he gave Zoe the chance to think about it that would be just what he would be doing. Looking back now, Al had to laugh about it. There wasn't ever a chance to tell Zoe she was wrong or that any of her ideas were crazy. Even if he did tell her he would have been put in his place pretty darn quickly. He remembered telling her once, when he was a

43

kid, that he felt his sock drawer was neat enough for her. He then spent the rest of the afternoon putting all of his clothes back into the drawers, neat enough to pass her inspection. That was Aunt Zoe in a nutshell and he loved her for it. That attention to detail, and wanting to please her, helped him through a lot of things in life, including his job. So that was how he ended up where he was now, on a deserted back road someplace in Illinois heading south toward Florida.

They couldn't try taking the highway because Zoe said there wasn't much chance of finding survivors there. Joe had tried to argue with her, having not been around Zoe as much as Al had been; he didn't know he had lost before he had ever started.

Al didn't see the truck coming from the side street as he worked his way around the abandoned cars. It was all he could do to just watch for any debris that might be in the road. At the last minute he saw something move in the corner of his eye. Letting his foot off the gas pedal and pushing the clutch in, he watched the truck go in front of him, stopping when it collided with a blue Honda abandoned on the side of the road. Pushing the brake in, turning the motor off, Al ran from the bus. Taking a quick look back toward the other bus, he motioned at Joe to come forward. Joe sprang out of the truck, running towards Al carrying an old hunting rifle that he had found during the last stop.

"What is it, Dad?" Joe asked out of breath.

Al shook his head and shrugged his shoulders. "Unless zombies can drive there may be a person in there."

They made their way closer to the truck; Al noticed that Joe was paying more attention to the goods in the bed of the truck than to whatever was driving it and back handed him lightly against the chest. Al motioned towards the cab, which brought a knowing nod from Joe. When they reached the window, they saw a young girl was slumped over the seat, covered in blood.

"Back up," Al said, "we don't know if she has been bitten or not. Maybe we should just drive on and put some distance between us and her."

Joe nodded in agreement with his father and backed away until he ran into someone causing him to jump, dropping the rifle.

"Aunt Zoe you scared the life out of me! What are you doing out here? I told you to stay in the bus!"

Zoe looked him in the eye with that un-approving look that he had been told so many times by his father about, and she said, "Boy, move out of my way!"

Joe slid out of her way, embarrassed about the whole exchange, as Zoe walked over to the truck door and looked in.

"This child is still alive! Pull her out of this truck so I can get a good look at her."

Al shook his head no; that was going too far when she was plainly going to put the rest of them in danger.

"I said come help me get this girl out of this truck! I didn't think I was talking to myself, Albert!"

Al gave in like he had his whole life and helped take the girl from the truck. There was so much blood that he couldn't tell where it was coming from.

"She has lost a lot of blood, Aunt Zoe," Al said to her. "I think she is a lost cause."

Zoe just kept poking and prodding around trying to find the wound. There was a nasty cut crossing her forehead, but it didn't look deep enough for the rest of the mess. She decided the top had to go if she was going to prevent anymore loss. Clipped to the back of her hip was a knife that she took from the hardware store in Wisconsin. Reaching back she unclipped it and placed the blade under the bottom of the shirt and ripped upwards toward the collar. *There it was*, Zoe thought, *if there wasn't so much blood I would have seen it right off.* Something had taken a chunk off the girl's muscle off of her shoulder, just above her breast.

"Joseph, run back to the bus and grab as many towels as you can carry." Noticing the boy still standing there, like a deer in headlights, she added, "I am not going to tell you again, boy. Move!"

Joe snapped out of his dazed state and ran towards the bus as fast as he could.

"Mind you, tell those children to stay put for now!"

"Aunt Zoe, we can't deal with anything like this. We don't have the equipment." Al stated.

47

Zoe went on to look at the wounds as if he wasn't there. It looked to her like the bleeding by the shoulder had stopped for the most part. She didn't know how it had stopped, but it had. The lesser wounds were another story; they were still bleeding fairly badly.

"Albert, I do believe she will live through this just fine. Where is that boy with those towels? While you're looking for him, grab me a jug of water and bring it back with you."

Al was nearly floored, there was no way he was leaving her alone with a possible soon-to-be zombie. "I will not leave you alone, Aunt Zoe. Not with this!"

"Why? You figuring if she changes you will run over there, grab that rifle and shoot her before she takes to biting me? Get me that water, please, and hurry Joseph up."

Al went to get the water; there wasn't any use in arguing with her right now. If the girl started looking worse off, he would put up a fight Aunt Zoe would not forget anytime soon. Deep down he knew that wasn't true. The only person who ever proved to be a match for Zoe was his grandmother.

With the towels and water, Zoe started cleaning up the blood and putting pressure on the wounds still bleeding. When she was satisfied, Zoe stood up and looked back at her boys, "Lord help them if anything happens to me; they are two lost souls." She smiled at Al and pointed towards the bus, "I think for tonight, just to be safe, she should be put in your bus. Doesn't hurt to be a little cautious while we are being merciful."

"I don't want to drive with her behind me like that; and with it getting dark, Joe will have to drive your bus."

Zoe understood that; she couldn't see so well anymore after dark, and there was no one Al would have to watch his back other than Joe. "We should sleep right here for now. We can leave her in that bus, and everyone bunk down in our bus."

For the first time since they ran across this girl, Zoe was making some sense to him now. Even though it was probably more her way of saying, 'OK, I understand your concerns, even if you are wrong.' Al didn't care; he would take that as a minor win. Any win with Aunt Zoe was a vote of confidence from her in your judgment. Not something earned easily.

"Joe, grab one of the pieces of plywood that we brought to put across the seats to make a bed. Put it across the very back seat so that we can see if she is lying there in the morning. I don't guess if she changes over night there is any possibility of her opening the door, and I don't want to get a surprise when I open it to go in."

Joe nodded his head as he took off to get the plywood. "Bedding, too?" he asked.

"Just a blanket for tonight," Aunt Zoe replied.

Zoe took in a long look at her nephew, remembering for a moment how glad she always had been to spend time with him. She was the one who would always tell him what was on her mind one way or another; good or bad. This was going to be one of those times when she had to let him know that he had disappointed her. Thinking a little longer about it she decided that maybe it hadn't been all that bad. Albert had spoken his mind when he thought she was endangering everyone. That was better than him letting her drive them off a cliff. Perhaps this whole 'end of the world thing' was finally toughening him up a little bit.

"Al, once you guys get her settled, I will have the children help me get a fire started so we can eat before it gets dark."

That was all she said to him as she passed him on the way back to the other bus. Al had known that look his whole life and it never ended that way before. Even while he was somewhat happy with himself he couldn't help but wonder if something was wrong with her.

****

Virginia watched them pull Lori from the truck and work on her wounds. Then saw them pick her up and take her into the lead bus. Perseus, watching intently, let out a moan seeing this.

"That's Ok boy, Lori isn't like us. She will do better with those people than she will alone with us."

For a moment Virginia truly believed that she felt that way. The pain of losing anyone else was not an option in her world right now, she told herself. There had been no tears since her mother was taken away and there would be none. Still, it was odd that they put Lori in one bus, while the rest went to the other. She watched silently as they cooked their food on an open fire made

51

in the middle of the highway. After eating they all retired to the inside of the bus and there was no more movement.

Sometime over the course of the evening Virginia decided she would see her sister one more time. The plan involved going after dark, which would have driven Bob nuts. She wasn't all that crazy about the idea herself, if she was being honest. Not giving herself away as being there right now, seemed to make it a little better. With the dogs, she would know if anything else was out there with her so it could be something she could pull off. Zeus and Perseus could keep watch while she went in the bus to say good bye to Lori. At least this time she would get to tell someone good bye.

CHAPTER 4

Most of the day had been overcast as a snowstorm came in from the northwest. The nights were so dark that Virginia couldn't even make out the buses on the street, let alone the farmhouse just off to the side of the barn. Having decided to say good bye to Lori was one thing; getting to Lori was another.

The safest way to get to Lori would be to go by route of the street. The quickest way would be to go across the field. The only problem with going that way would be the dogs. Virginia had never really thought about the fence along the highway. Would she have to climb it or she could simply step through it? The more she thought about it the less of an option it became. Being brave with the dogs in pitch black night she could do; being brave without, not so much.

Having had the decision made for her, Virginia gathered up the few things she wanted to bring with her. Mainly the crossbow, arrows, and an emergency flair she had found. Leading the way downstairs it was comforting to see Zeus moving like his old self. Today was such a scare, that for an instant, Virginia thought about leaving him in the safety of the barn. Perseus could handle himself should anything come up; there was no doubt about that. What he couldn't do without Zeus was avoid falling back into being a puppy, and Virginia couldn't risk that at night.

Zeus led the way past the house and down the street; Perseus stayed next to Virginia's side. Once her eyes adjusted to the lack of light, she could make out Zeus in the lead, moving slow and steady down the middle of the street. The whole time it seemed like her heartbeat was so loud that it could be heard from a mile away. She felt only a little relief when the gravel beneath her feet transitioned to pavement. From there they were very near the buses.

As they approached the first bus, Virginia felt for the door and lightly pushed it open. As the door folded into itself, Virginia shook her head and wondered if the door to the other bus would open so easily. If there were any two's nearby they would be in this in an instant.

Telling the dogs to stay, she loaded an arrow into the crossbow and climbed the stairs. Unfortunately, like the strangers, she had no idea if Lori had changed or not. For now it seemed being safer was the proper thing to do, no matter who it was in the bus.

At the top of the stairs she could hear Lori breathing heavy from the back of the bus. With each step she wondered if her sister would make it. Knowing that if she had been bitten that she would not survive didn't stop her from thinking about it. When she had reached the make shift bed, Lori's figure could barely be made out. She didn't know if Lori would make it, but she could tell easily that she had not turned. She didn't even sound like she was in process of turning.

Virginia placed the back of her hand on Lori's jaw and held it there for a few minutes, until the first tear tried to escape from her eyes. She wanted to check the other bus out, to see if it was better locked down than Lori's had been.

"Perseus, come on boy, guard Lori," she called out to Perseus as she climbed down out of the bus. Once he was inside Virginia pulled the door closed as best she could.

Zeus led the way to the other bus and stopped in front of the door. Once again Virginia lightly pushed the door into an open position and then froze to see if she could hear any movement inside. Hearing none, she once again climbed the steps with the crossbow at the ready. Once at the top she stood there listening again for movement. The only sounds were a light snoring and the normal, deep breathing of sleep.

"Zeus," she called out and Zeus went up the stairs as Virginia pushed the lever, closing the doors.

The air grew colder as the sun came up and the first to stir looked up into Virginia's eyes and the crossbow aimed at them. He made a sudden reach for his rifle and then thought better of it.

"Joey, if she wanted to kill us we would all be dead by now," Aunt Zoe stated.

Virginia made a shush signal with her finger raised to her lips, and pointed outside. There were around ten zombies, milling around the area where the fire had been. Virginia could see the look of alarm in their eyes when they turned back towards her. In a low voice she said, "Whatever you do, don't shoot that rifle off now."

"He doesn't have any bullets," Zoe replied, causing Virginia to smile at the thought of carrying a gun around with no bullets in it.

"They will move on unless we give them a reason to stay."

Zoe and Joey nodded their heads that they understood.

Looking over the contents of the bus Virginia felt sorry for them. There were little or no supplies to be seen. They all looked like they were as cold as she was, despite the blankets wrapped around them. If she needed more proof that everyone left alive was just walking dead and did not yet know that they were dead, this bunch was it.

"Can anyone tell me why this girl is on the bus pointing an arrow at us?" Al asked in a groggy voice as he wiped the sleep from his eyes.

"That would be a good question, Albert," Zoe replied, "Well?"

"I came down to say good bye to my sister. I saw you put her in that other bus," Virginia replied.

"You mean when we saved your sister, don't you?" Joe asked

"Will she live?" Virginia asked Zoe.

Zoe looked into Virginia's face then closed her eyes and shook her head no, "I really don't know, child. We don't have any medicines to give her."

"We have them back at the bunker and it is a lot warmer there, or could be, than it is here."

"How old are you girl?" Al asked looking concerned.

"I will be fourteen in a month--if I am still alive. Who knows with the way things are if I will make that or not."

Al didn't like the fact that this girl seemed to be holding all of the cards right now. He had a very specific plan to reach Florida. Contrary to what Aunt Zoe kept saying, that plan didn't include picking up wounded people with troubled children. This child here was going to be a lot of trouble one way or the other he thought.

"If you're planning on staying here, this bus is in a bad place," Virginia added. "You might want to move it off of this main road and hunker down for a few hours."

To prove her point Virginia pointed back up the road at the zombies. What had been a few milling about aimlessly was now up to about twenty or thirty, moving more directly.

"They stick to roads mostly when they move in large groups. We have always called them herds when their numbers get higher."

They moved closer to the windows to get a better look. The girl was right about the numbers going up. It was like they were at a gathering spot waiting for others to join them.

"How many have you seen together?" Zoe asked.

"So many that it has looked like a river of dead moving slowly past."

Al sat back down in his seat and bit his lower lip the way he had while in deep thought since he was a little boy. "I think we will be safe in the bus," he stated.

"You will look like a packaged meal, but, suit yourself," Virginia replied.

"What do you mean, child?" Zoe asked.

Virginia put down her crossbow and petted Zeus's head. Without looking up she said, "Picture this bus surrounded by the dead for as far as the eye can see. When you can see that in your head take a few minutes and imagine that same group hungry. When you have imagined that, picture five alive, and moving creatures in this bus. Now when you can see all of that you just need to put it all together."

Al may not have been able to see what she was talking about, but Zoe saw it plain as day. They would be trapped inside the bus with little food and less water for who knows how long.

"This place of yours would be safe for all of us?" Zoe asked.

Virginia thought about it a few minutes. The truth was that she didn't know for sure what they would find back at the bunker. Lori had been there and looks like she had barely gotten away. It was a bad sign that there had been no sign of the others. Not even the smoke from the chimney was visible.

"If it is clear, there is no place safer that I can think of. We would have to go take a look before moving everyone there."

"Good, we will all just wait here for you and your dog to get back," Al added.

"I don't think you should stay on the road. Maybe you could move over by the farm house or into the barn," Virginia said pointing towards the farm.

Al looked the farm over and got an idea. Why couldn't they just wait out this "herd" in the farm?

"Maybe that is a good spot to hold out at," he said finally.

"You can do whatever you think is best for you guys. I like to pick places that there aren't a lot of places for them to find a way in. They are not very smart, but they do seem to stumble upon weak spots when they want in."

Zoe was losing her patience with Al mentally fencing with this girl. From what she could see outside of the bus, they were losing precious time.

"OK child, what do you suggest we do?" Zoe asked.

Virginia thought for a few seconds then said, "We should take the vehicles over to the farm for now. I think we can fit one of them inside the barn to keep you and the

61

children safe. Then we can take the truck over to the bunker and make sure it is clear. Once we know it is clear, or have cleared it, we come back here to get you guys and my sister."

She looked at Zoe, Al, and Joe for their reaction. Seeing the lost looks on their faces made Virginia wonder if she was going to regret helping them out.

Al finally shook his head no, "This is all crazy!"

"Albert let's just get the buses moved and take a look at her place. We know what is behind us; you can see them plain as day. I don't know what is ahead of us, and neither do you. Right now the safe bet would be to follow our new friend here, so get us moving!"

"Why don't we just drive to her place and cut out the farm then?" Al asked.

"Bob didn't design the entrance to fit buses. The last thing we want is to be stuck back there with no way out other than walking."

"Fine! Joe, you drive this bus and I will take the other."

"What about the truck? Do you want to walk from the farm back there? Virginia asked.

"Joey, you drive that truck with the girl and her dog. Albert, you drive the other bus and I will drive this one," Zoe stated.

Al wasn't happy but it was settled as far as he was concerned. They would move the buses and go see how great this place was. Then tomorrow he would talk to Zoe about leaving this girl and her sister behind once and for all. Good riddance to them!

Moving the buses to the farm took a little longer than Virginia had hoped. The herd was growing steadily by now on the main road, with smaller groups visible in the fields to the north of them.

Virginia didn't want to tell them just yet that the bunker was to the north. The north of the bunker was mostly lake with the exception of the narrow strip of land heading to the northeast. She thought the two point zeroes had moved through there at times. It was starting to get darker outside and she did not want to run into them tonight with this group out in the open.

"Ok, we are moved here. What's next?" Al asked her.

"We can move my sister into the bus with them in the barn. They can latch the door from the inside and stay inside the bus, or go to the loft, until we get back."

Zoe shook her head in agreement as she walked over to her nephew and great-nephew. "You two be careful and we will see you real soon," she said as she hugged both of them.

"Don't worry. We will be with the little General," Al replied smartly.

Virginia opened the tailgate and called out, "Lads, get in." The two dogs jumped up into the bed of the truck and she shut the tailgate.

"Do they have to come too?" Al asked her.

"Trust me. You will be glad they are with us."

Al didn't like big dogs or small dogs. He didn't care how much he may need them; he just didn't trust any dog to not bite him.

They drove down the road fast enough to move at a good speed, but slow enough to not attract the herd too much. When they reached the gate, Virginia's heart sank noticing the gate was open and remembered that she had left it that way just a day before. Albert stopped at the gate and looked to her for answers. Virginia looked back at him and then turned to Joe sitting to her left by the passenger door.

"Can you please close and latch the gate after we drive through?"

He shook his head yes and Al drove through the gate, stopping just the on other side. Virginia got out with Joe and let the dogs out of the bed. Returning to the cab with the lads she reached into the storage space behind the seat and pulled out two pistols, laying them on the seat. Taking the safety off the first one, she handed it carefully to Al. Then did the same with the other and handed it to Joe.

"Sound attracts them more than anything else. Do NOT shoot anything unless you absolutely have too, OK?"

They both nervously nodded their heads.

"The lads will lead the way, if anything is in there or near us, they will stop us." Looking into Al's eyes first and then into Joe's, Virginia could see how afraid they both were right now. She hoped that they wouldn't do anything stupid and get them all killed.

"You follow slowly in the truck, keeping an eye on me and the dogs. If anything pops up I will get it with the crossbow or the dogs will get it; are you following me? This is life or death now. There is no room for you two to freak out or do something stupid." Moving out of the way she motioned for Joe to get into the truck. Once they were inside and the truck door shut, Virginia took one more look at her two new partners. Satisfied that they knew what to do, and more importantly, not to do, she joined the dogs.

Raising the crossbow up, Virginia followed the lads toward the open bunker door, pausing for a few seconds where she had last sat with Bob. From there she could see the door better and the remains of Jack, by the trailer. The hair on Zeus' back raised and then Perseus followed suit. Zeus fell back and crossed his body in front of Virginia, letting out a low growl. Hearing this, Perseus moved in front of her as well, into a defensive position.

Patting Zeus on the head she whispered, "What's in there boy?"

Zeus moved forward ready to strike the strange smell coming from inside the bunker.

Virginia reached into her back pocket and pulled out the flare she had been carrying. Striking it, the flare roared to life in a tremendous white glow. Walking up to where Zeus now stood, she could hear the unmistakable labored breathing of the zombies inside the bunker.

In the dark they had the advantage; in the light she would take them down as they exited the bunker to get away from the flare. She tossed the flare through the door and raised the crossbow, waiting.

The inside of the bunker lit up in a reddish, white glow as the flare landed near the fire place. The labored breath turned to horrifying growls emanating from the bunker. With a burst of movement they surged through the door, trying to escape the flare. Virginia let the arrow go, striking the first one in the left eye. Zeus brought the second zombie down while she loaded the next arrow, striking the third one. Perseus lunged for a fourth, and Virginia brought down the last to emerge.

The zombie in Zeus's grasp was trying unsuccessfully to break free of the vice like jaw clamped on his neck. While Zeus was doing his best to bite clean through the neck it looked like Perseus was playing with his; letting it go, then pouncing on it again as if to show that he was the master of the creature's fate. Only when Virginia shot it in the head with an arrow did Perseus let it go. Wondering if Zeus could really bite through the neck, Virginia decided to end that one too, similarly.

Virginia glanced back at Al and Joe as she followed the lads into the bunker. The flare's glow lit the main room fairly well, even if it was starting to burn down. Virginia flipped the light switch by the door hoping that the solar batteries had been charged enough. The lights responded, bathing the room in light. Walking over to the flare, Virginia picked it up and tossed it into the fireplace. Zeus's relaxed posture told her that the bunker was cleared of any danger. Out of habit she went from room to room verifying it for herself; not that she didn't trust the lads at all. On the contrary, she would trust Zeus and Perseus with her life before she would trust anyone else.

Once she was sure it was safe, she went out to get Al and Joe; reminding them to bring the pistols with them, and to shut the truck doors. Virginia gave them a quick tour of the bunker, pausing only when she thought one or both of them were going to vomit.

"We can't bring the children in here with this," Al said pointing at Bob's corpse.

Virginia thought for a few minutes about what could be done with the bodies, then came up with an idea, "We can drag them out to the garbage pile for today."

Al didn't want to touch them at all, and Zoe would never let them throw the bodies away like trash. "We can't just throw them away like last night's pizza box," Al replied.

"We can leave them there for tonight, and you can do what you want to do with them tomorrow."

Nodding his agreement, Al motioned for Joe to help him get the bodies out of the bunker. Virginia loaded an arrow and followed them. She repeated this as they moved Julie's remains to the garbage pile. Then again as the zombies were being dragged. Finally, Joe asked her, "Are you going to help or just follow us around?"

"I thought you might want me to cover you in case something came out of the woods, or from behind the wood shed. I don't have to if it bothers you that much."

"Joe help me get this last one over there and leave her be. I feel better with her and that bow watching my back," Al stated, smiling over at her.

Once the last body was thrown onto the pile Virginia went back into the bunker and turned all of the lights off but a small one in the main room. They would need to conserve the batteries until Al or Joe could get the generator going tomorrow. On leaving the bunker she latched the sole outside latch on the massive steel door. Joe opened the tailgate to let the dogs back into the bed of the truck without being told to by Virginia.

"It will be dark soon, do you think we can fit everyone in one trip?" Virginia asked.

Joe shrugged his shoulders as he got into the truck. "Maybe one of us should stay here?"

Al shook his head no, and said, "We need her to keep our way clear while you and I carry her sister. We will fit everyone somehow."

Virginia swung the massive gate open then pulled it closed after Al drove the truck through. Walking back to the cab she pictured the gate being open when they had left yesterday. Virginia didn't know if the feelings welling up inside her were fear of being found out or sorrow. Zeus and Perseus were becoming agitated in the back of the truck, helping her find her way back to the reality of the moment. Pausing, Virginia stared into the darkness at a fixed point. Her mind searched for any movement in the shadows; a sign that something was there that shouldn't be. When she had decided that nothing was there, she climbed into the truck. The whole drive back was silent; no one seemed to have anything to say, which suited Virginia just fine. She was trying to listen for any sounds out of the dogs over the truck's engine. She knew no better early warning system than Zeus and Perseus.

When they reached the farm they could all see a light on inside. Al stopped the truck and said, "Who do you think would have left the barn?"

"Aunt Zoe," Joe replied, and they both chuckled because if anyone did, it would have been Zoe. Zoe had a way of doing what she wanted, when she wanted, and they both knew that.

"Stop the truck over there, between the barn and house," Virginia instructed.

Al brought the truck to a slow glide into the place where Virginia had been pointing to. She eased the door open and motioned for them to head towards the barn. Zeus and Perseus jumped down out of the bed and took up their positions on either side of Virginia as they once again headed up the stairs to the farm house. The door burst inward, opening to reveal the largest man Virginia had ever seen standing there with what looked like a steak knife. The lads moved in front of Virginia snarling at the man.

"We don't want any troubles. If this is your house we're sorry, but we need a place to stay for the night. The man waited for an answer, and when he saw that none was coming he continued, "We have children in here, and they need to get warmed up."

From off to her left side, standing next to the porch, a voice came, "Bring everyone outside and let us see them."

Virginia took her eyes off the man for a second to see if it could possibly be who she thought it was. Sure enough, standing there with her crossbow aimed at the door was Lori! Lori, who she had thought would possibly pass before the night was out was standing there.

"OK, give me a second please, need to get the kids moving."

A few minutes later a much smaller man came out carrying a child, followed by a woman also carrying one. Then came a smaller, skinnier woman followed by the large man.

"OK we're all out here. What next?"

"Move from the door, off to the right, and remember I have an arrow aimed at your head. No funny business or you're the first to go," Lori replied.

"There will be no funny business. Move over there ya'll," the man said as he pushed the group over.

"Zeus. Perseus. Go check it out," Lori commanded the two dogs.

The lads disappeared into the house for a few minutes then came back out and sat facing the strangers.

Lori lowered her crossbow and told the group to follow her. They walked past the dogs, and then Virginia, until they caught up with Lori. "Move quickly and quietly. I think you attracted a few things I would rather not meet up with right now. Best to be gone when they make it here."

When they reached the barn door the group found themselves facing Zoe, Al and Joe. All three were armed, thanks to Virginia, and not giving an inch.

"They are ok, you don't need those right now," Lori stated. "Besides, if they try anything the dogs will take care of them before we even know what's going on."

"I believe that," Al said lowering the pistol. He looked over at Zoe and nodded his head towards Lori questioningly.

"She got up a little while after you guys left. Seems to be ok, considering."

"Zoe, I don't know why that surprises me after spending time with the little General there," he remarked as he smiled at Virginia, getting a rare return smile from her. "We should get everyone over to their bunker where it is warm."

Lori's face went pale, "No! You can't go there! There is…"

Al, stopped her and said, "Don't you worry about anything being in there. Your sister and those big dogs went in there like the Marines landing on a beach. It is all clear for us civilians now."

****

CHAPTER 5

The ride back was silent for Charlie, even though Doc was talking a mile a minute. Words couldn't really explain what he had just seen. It was like a horrible nightmare that just wouldn't end. There was no way in hell that this could be what Annie had turned into. Someplace inside of that thing was the woman who loved him more than anything else. He would walk through fire for Annie, and there was no doubt in Charlie's mind that she would for him. If Doc was expecting him to just throw away years of happiness and pull the plug on any hopes of being with Annie again, there was a sad awakening coming fairly soon.

Doc pulled into Charlie's driveway and Charlie swung the door open. He climbed out in a daze while trying to put everything he had seen together. All the afternoon's sights raced around in an endless loop. Always starting with, and returning to, Annie before it raced through again.

"Charlie," Doc said, "I know you don't want this, but take it anyway." Doc handed him the sheriff's forty-five. "If you won't take it for you; take it so I feel a little better."

Charlie reached out and took the handgun, knowing full well that he wouldn't use it on Annie. Watching Doc pull away, he swung the front door open. The smell in the house was a little like the Sheriff's office had smelled, but not as strong. Charlie set the gun down on the antique table just inside the door, then made his way to Annie's bright-red living room furniture.

Sitting down on the sofa he could hear rumbling coming from their bedroom. Rumbling that quickly turned to crashing, followed by what Charlie would have sworn was a low guttural roar.

If asked, Charlie couldn't say how long he had been sitting there listening to the ruckus in the room above. Time had passed quickly, considering that his mind had all but stopped. It wasn't until the afternoon shadow started to form through the windows that his mind was finally made up. Life without Annie wasn't life. It was a slow death filled with pain and remorse. If there was a way to reach her, Charlie had to try. He owed her that much; He owed them that much.

Starting up the stairs, he paused on the third step and looked at the gun on the table. As if it was just a passing thought, Charlie continued up. The scent grew stronger with every step, but the sound had died down to nearly nothing. Deep inside he hoped that she had worn herself out, making this a little easier to do. At the door he listened for any sounds of movement before inserting the makeshift key that came with all of the locks. There was a faint click as the key released the tumblers of the lock. Pushing the door inward, the view of the room grew from a narrow strip to a wide view of everything but the far wall. The antique dresser that Annie had loved so much was shattered into pieces, along with the matching makeup table. Charlie took a deep breath and entered the room, keeping his eyes toward the unseen wall. There, in the near corner, was Annie with her head pressed against the crook of the wall. Charlie gathered his courage and called out her name slightly more audible than a whisper. No response. Moving a little closer and calling out again, he managed a little louder this time. Annie pulled her head from the wall and looked back over her shoulder at Charlie. Her eyes were no longer a beautiful emerald green, but black as coal and sunken in. Creamy white skin had turned to a pale sickly gray and her lips had pulled back exposing her teeth.

Before Charlie had knew it, Annie was across the room and on top of him. Her grasp was stronger than any he had ever felt, as she tried to pull him closer. Instinctively, his arms pushed back at the lunging body. A hand had hold of each of Charlie's shoulders while Annie's teeth were clicking in anticipation of feeding. Pushing against her neck with every ounce of strength in him only seemed to keep the teeth from finding their mark. Around the master bedroom they circled until Charlie somehow broke free. As Annie started forward Charlie grabbed the light that had once been on the night stand on his side of the bed, and brought it crashing into Annie's side, knocking her off kilter for a few seconds before the advance started again. It was then that it had finally sunk in for Charlie. Now was the moment to decide his fate once and for all: let Annie end it all so that there was no having to go on without her, or make a hasty retreat from the room. This is not the way Charlie was going to go out, he decided, as he brought the lamp back up against the side of her head, sending the creature back, sprawling onto the floor. Charlie slowly backed out of the room as Annie worked her way to her feet.

On the way out, Charlie left the door open because if Doc was right, these creatures couldn't climb stairs. At the bottom of the stairs he tried to catch his breath and decide what he would take with him. Clothing was kind of out of the question now, unless it was in the laundry room. His coat, shoes and some food to last a few days were all down here.

A sudden crashing sound caused him to leap to his feet, swinging around. Doc said they couldn't climb stairs, but he never mentioned falling down them. Annie was lying on the landing, growling and hissing at him. Later, Charlie would say he thought it was more of a hiss, but that the growl had definitely been there too. She began a slow decent by crawling and falling down the last flight. Reaching for the gun on the table and raising it up in front of him Charlie said, "Stop! I don't want to shoot you Annie! Just stop!" She kept coming, no more than three steps left before the main floor. Charlie squeezed the trigger and the round found its way into what had been Annie's head. In the silence that followed, their life together passed in front of Charlie's eyes. Of the millions of things that could have gone

wrong in their marriage to bring it to an end,
this was not one he had ever feared.
Dropping the gun to the floor, Charlie went
out of the front door and sat down.

******

Everyone climbed into the bed of
the truck with the exception of Al,
Virginia and Joe, who all rode in the
cab. The road was dark, with shadows
moving everywhere along the side.
When one seemed to be a little too far
towards the center of the road for
comfort, Al would veer toward the
other side, never going too far for fear
of what could be there unseen. As they
pulled up to the gate the anxiety level
rose as the truck slowly stopped and
Virginia climbed out. Lori jumped down
from the bed and called the lads to her
side. "Go ahead, Virginia, open the
gate. We are clear for the moment."
Without question, Virginia unlatched
the gate and swung it open. Al drove
through at a slow but constant pace
with Virginia and Lori following. As
Virginia swung the gate closed, Lori
sent the lads ahead to check out the
entrance to the bunker. Perseus circled
the area a few times sniffing

81

everything, while Zeus moved up to the door and smelled the air in all directions. Finding no danger present, he sat down facing the truck while Perseus, also finding it safe, continued to run around in circles. Lori came up and unlatched the door, motioning everyone inside. As Jermaine passed she motioned him to follow her, leading him to the generator.

"I'm going to prime this. Could you flip that switch please?"

Lori gave the primer three quick pumps and pointed a finger at Jermaine. Flipping the switch, Jermaine stepped back as the generator roared to life.

"Will this call out to the creatures?"

"It will quiet down in a few minutes. Besides, I think they know we are here," Lori replied. "Let's go make sure everyone is inside all the same, and get everything closed up for the night."

CHAPTER 6

The night had passed fitfully with very little sleep to be had for Lori. Every time she had managed to feel as if she were asleep the horrible dead face would reappear, once again leering down at her as it scooped hunks of flesh from her shoulder. Giving up, Lori quietly made her way out of the sleeping area towards the warm glow of the fire in the great room. Starting towards the kitchenette to make a pot of coffee Lori stopped at Bob's truck sitting against the wall. Bob never thought of the bunker as a permanent place to stay. It was just one stop on a list of places he felt were safe enough to hold up at. Opening the truck, Lori quickly found the tattered old folder that Bob kept his maps in. The first was a large map with all of the stops circled in red. Underneath that was a local map for each and every red circle on the larger map.

Laying the large map out on the table Lori traced the red line from the bunker to a place called Rivers Crossing. It didn't look like much of a place on the large map, and even less of a place on the local map. Of course, when she thought about it, the bunker didn't look like much either from the maps and it started out reasonably well.

"I didn't figure you for an early riser," Zoe stated, startling Lori a little.

"I was having a hard time sleeping so I decide to just go with it," Lori replied smiling.

Zoe walked up to Lori and pointed at her shoulder, "You really should let me have a look at that."

Lori nodded ok and pulled the shirt up over the shoulder. Zoe could see the wound was all but healed. If not for the gray glassy look the skin had turned you wouldn't even be able to tell that there had been a serious wound there. Poking it softly Zoe added "It is hard as a rock, does that hurt?"

"It feels odd, but it doesn't hurt there. I have more pain in the red areas around it."

Zoe pulled the shirt back down over the shoulder and said, "For right now let's keep this between you and I, ok?" Lori nodded her head in agreement.

Zoe started to explain her reasons but thought better of it for now and changed the subject. "So what are all these maps for?"

"I don't think we are safe here anymore."

"This place seems pretty safe; almost like a fort," Zoe replied.

"Inside here we are as safe as anyplace, that's for sure. Outside I feel like something is coming towards us that will make it unsafe. We can't stay in here forever; we will need to get supplies from out there."

"So where do we go that will be safe then?" Jermaine asked.

Lori and Zoe didn't notice that most of the group had come into the room and begun listening quietly.

"If you look at this map here," Lori said pointing to the main map, "Bob, the man who built and stocked the bunker we are in now, was a pretty good prepper. He had planned on making his way to a place that he felt would be a safe place to wait until things settled down. This is just the first place on the map, as you can see."

Al pointed toward an island circled in red off of the east coast of Florida, "So we pack up and go here then? Has to be the safest spot if it is the last one."

"Bob would never do that!" Virginia interrupted.

"No, he wouldn't," Lori added, "Each spot on this map will probably have much needed supplies with a safe place to hold up, and get some rest for a few days."

"So you just want us to blindly follow a mapped out plan made by a guy we never knew?" Al asked.

"I am not here to tell anyone what they should, or should not do. You all have to do as you see best for you and your families. We are going to follow Bob's map and you're all welcome to come along, if you want."

"I, for one, am not following two girls into the unknown. We could easily take those maps and everything else," Roy stated as he headed towards the table. Zeus, hearing the tone in his voice, advanced between Roy and the table, bearing his fangs as he sat down facing Roy. If that didn't help Roy get the point, Perseus seemed to purposely knock into Roy as he took his place next to Zeus, ready to pounce. Roy eased himself back behind his wife and children.

"Mister, I do believe you just made the best decision of your life," Al chuckled.

Zoe started to add to it but stopped when she felt Lori gently squeeze her hand. "No one has to come with us. You can stay here or go where ever you want to go. The choice is yours and yours alone. We will split all of the supplies up on a per person basis."

"If you and the little general are going, we're going with you," Al stated, looking at Zoe for confirmation.

She responded with a nod.

Jermaine smiled and said "I believe Taquisha and I will stay with you guys for a while." Pam quickly echoed that sentiment, then added as she turned to face her husband, "Anyone not agreeing can find their own way!" Roy got the point and smiled as he nodded his head that he was, of course, in.

******

87

Judging by the sun it was late afternoon, Charlie thought to himself. Sitting there, time had no meaning to him anymore. Had it not been for the noise of a large truck coming from Main Street he probably would have still been sitting there in his own world. Hearing it reminded him that Doc was at the new school, in town, with a few other survivors. Pulling himself off the stoop, Charlie started walking toward Main Street. Growing up Charlie had always wondered if one day Rivers Crossing would turn into a ghost town. The thought kept popping up as he walked through the dead streets. The houses all appeared to be empty. All that was missing was a tumble weed blowing down the street, and a door slamming shut in the breeze.

Reaching Main Street, Charlie could see Doc standing in front of the school watching the dump truck back up to the ramp with a small group of people. He walked towards them, looking forward to being around others.

"Charlie! I was just going to come out and check on you when that pulled up over there," Doc said pointing towards the truck.

"Do we know who that is?"

"Not a clue, Charlie. I was hoping you would know the truck,' Doc replied.

"Let's go see who it is then, Doc. Is that loaded?" Charlie asked pointing at the gun in Doc's holster.

"Wouldn't be of much use if it wasn't, now would it, Charlie?"

The closer they moved towards the old school Charlie thought that the dump truck looked a little familiar, but he still could not match it to an owner yet.

"Where is your gun at, Charlie? The one I gave you this morning when I dropped you off?"

"I dropped it when I had to…" Charlie felt like he was going to start crying; all of his strength drained from his legs. "I just dropped it someplace," Charlie finished with his voice cracking.

"Sorry, Charlie, I knew it was coming, but didn't know how to tell you," Doc replied.

Charlie didn't want to talk about the subject but forced himself to say, "I guess I knew too, Doc, after your little tour this morning."

They didn't say anything more as they walked up the stairs to the school yard.

"Good morning! An elderly man said from next to the dump truck. Charlie recognized him right off as Boo Peterson. His name was Beau Peterson, but all of the children in town, including Charlie, grew up knowing him as Boo Peterson. He was a cautionary tale told to bad children that stayed outside too late after dark. Charlie could remember well the tales his mom would tell him. "Better get in here. It's starting to get dark outside. You don't want old Boo Peterson to catch you and cut your ears off for his collection do you?"

"I am glad you fellas came over. I was going to stop by you after I got these supplies stowed away," Boo stated. "Come on inside and let me show you around the old place,"

Once inside the first thing Charlie noticed was how warm and clean it was. The heat took your breath away compared to the dropping temperatures outside.

"I am sure you fellas noticed the heat?" Boo asked. "The old girl has a coal boiler, with plenty of coal to spare, keeping her warm and toasty. Our late mayor thought he might be able to repurpose or sell her; the last thing he wanted was to have the cold weather damage anything. If we run out of coal, there is plenty more to be found on the coal train that runs into Bixby, feeding the electric company. It just happens to be stopped on the south end of my farm. It has been there for about three weeks or so, I would guess. I noticed the other morning that there were survivors and that you were gathering them at the new school over there. It is a nice enough building, with its modern open concept, I guess. If you're going to gather up what is left of the town I think this old girl is perfect for the task. First of all, it has heat. Not just a bunch of propane heaters that you know will not last or do the trick come the real cold," Boo paused, letting it sink in. "The old girl was built as part of the "New Deal" during the depression. Back then there was a thought that Rivers Crossing would grow into a decent sized town with the river traffic and the train depot. They built the school and the library, which was later repurposed as the town hall. The old girl and the library is built seven feet higher than the normal grade. That was because of the yearly river flooding back before they built the dam a few miles upriver. I can tell you that it was a godsend a few springs, when the whole town was able to take shelter in these two buildings. That extra seven feet makes it a decent place to defend against what is out there."

Doc looked around at all of the supplies that Boo had dumped onto the school yard. "What is all of this for?"

Boo looked Doc in the eye, then Charlie, then back to Doc. "This is to keep the creatures out of this yard. We can close off almost all the entrances by shutting the gates and chaining them. This stuff is to reinforce them."

"A little overkill, don't you think?" Doc asked

"Boy, you young fellas haven't been outside of town have you? Follow me please," Boo stated.

They followed him down the hallway to the back stairway and started up. At the top of the stairs, off to the left, was a locked door that read, "Employees only." Boo unlocked the door and motioned the two younger men to follow again. The stairs rose up another flight ending at a door. Beyond the door they found themselves on the flat roof of the school. Boo pointed off to the west, towards the Van Buren farm. "You see that moving around there?"

"It looks like old man Van Buren's cattle herd?" Charlie asked.

Boo laughed so hard he thought he was going to pee himself. "No sir, that isn't cattle moving around on that farm. That is what I am aiming to keep off the school yard."

"Doc, I think you should take this man up on his offer and move everyone over here," Charlie stated.

"I think I agree with you, Charlie! Mr. Peterson, where do you want everyone at?"

"Look fellas, I am not in charge of anything. I am just the building caretaker, and I want to stay with you guys here. You decide what needs to be done, Charlie," Boo stated.

Both men looked at Charlie, waiting for him to decide. "Ok, for now, Doc. After everyone is settled in I am leaving town, just so you know." Charlie paused to see if they both understood then continued, "To start, let's move everyone and everything over from the new school into the warmth."

CHAPTER 7

After a good breakfast and a little
light hearted conversation Lori rose and
started unlatching the bunker door's three
heavy latches. The lads made their way in
front of her as she pulled the heavy door
open. Unconsciously, Lori moved to the side
and let them exit the bunker first. A few feet
from the safety of the bunker Zeus stopped
and sniffed the air while Perseus took
interest with the area by the trailer. Lori
stepped out of the door and began sniffing
the air as well. She also noticed the scent
coming from the area that Perseus was
preoccupied with. Her first thought was to
wonder why Zeus hadn't picked up the scent
as well. Oddly, it wasn't why she could pick
up scent and Zeus couldn't.

Virginia was close behind her and
noticed that Lori was sniffing the air much
the way that the lads did. Not wanting
anyone else to notice this odd behavior, she
said, "Zeus and Perseus, go check out the
trailer." With that the lads were both off
towards the trailer in an instant. Virginia
pushed Lori out from in front of the door
where no one could see her. "If you think it

is safe enough, maybe we should start loading up supplies."

Lori shook her head yes, and started toward the trailer as well. She knew that there was a question inside of what Virginia had said to her. She also knew that she didn't have an answer for it right now. Ever since she was attacked by the zombie, something inside of her had changed. Until she could explain it to herself there wasn't much sense in trying to explain it to anyone else.

"Come back, lads!" Lori commanded the dogs. "Virginia, you're right. We need to get started. We don't have a lot of time." Lori flipped her the truck keys, "Back the truck up to the door and see if you can find a good spot for you and the lads to watch over us." Virginia caught the keys and gave Lori a funny look. "Come on Virginia, everyone knew that Bob was teaching you how to drive the truck," Lori said smiling at her little sister. Virginia smiled back and went to get the truck.

"Something wrong?" Al asked as he came out. Virginia ignored him for a second and asked Jermaine as he was coming out, "You were off to the west, right?"

"Yea, we came from over East Moline," Jermaine replied.

"Where did you first run into the large herd?"

"I think it was a little town called Frankfort, or Frankfort Square. If you have a map I think I can show you," Jermaine replied.

"Try to think real hard. What was the herd doing?"

"Besides trying to get into the car and eat us?" Jermaine asked.

"When you first noticed them, what were they doing? Were they on the move?"

"It seemed like they were moving to the east. We drove into them, more or less."

"We ran into them coming from the Northwest. It would seem like they are going someplace, wouldn't it?" Lori asked.

"I think you're giving them more credit for intelligence than they deserve," Al said.

Jermaine thought for a minute and then agreed with Al, "Yea, from what I have seen, Al is right. They don't act like they have a lot of smarts."

"Not all of them, but some seem pretty smart in an animalistic way. Smart like a wolf pack hunting its prey,"

"I'll give you that. So what are you trying to say? Because I am not following you," Al asked.

"I think we need to get the supplies loaded, and get on the move. I have a bad feeling that something is coming; we don't want to be here when it gets here," Lori stated.

"I don't know you very well, but from what I have seen I will trust your judgment. I will get Joey and that other fella and get started now," Al replied.

As they started into the bunker Jermaine laughed and pointed towards Virginia and the lads, "What are they supposed to be doing out there?"

Al stopped and looked, "I don't really know but I would take her out there with that crossbow and the dogs over just about anyone else."

It didn't take long at all for them to fill the bed of the truck with supplies. Zoe came forward and dictated what went on the truck first, and where it should go when they reached the barn. She wanted the bulk of the medicine to be in the bus with a small amount of each in the RV. Once that was done, she wanted ammunition and the firearms to be divided up between the truck, bus, and the RV. That way, she had explained, if they lost any one vehicle they wouldn't lose all of their supplies. After that came the food, against Al's protestations. Al didn't think there was a reason to carry most of the food and waste space that could be used for water; not until Lori had interjected that there was a good chance a lot of the perishable foods would be rotten by now. Lori understood foraging in unknown homes when much of what they might find would be rotten and put them at risk was not the right move. Brining along all they could was far safer. Once that ran out they would form teams to search houses.

After the last of what they could take was loaded, Zoe herded everyone into the RV except Al, Lori, and Virginia. They would ride in the truck and lead the way to the barn, where Jermaine would be waiting with Joey and the bus. Once there the thought was they would have a few minutes to decide who would ride where, and how they would rotate drivers.

The move from the new school to the old school was going well, with few difficulties. Charlie noticed that most of the survivors looked like they were a living version of the zombies. They went through the motions of moving around, but their eyes and facial expressions were blank. Many, Charlie thought, probably had to do what he had done this morning just to survive in this hell. He also noticed, when he talked to them, or had even walked by them, they seemed to come to life just a little bit. Probably because he had known most of them his whole life.

Boo Peterson saw Charlie watching the last of the move and walked over to him, extending his hand. Charlie shook his hand not knowing why, other than it was a warm greeting to another human being.

"I think I have a way to secure the yard for the night. It isn't anything to keep permanent, but it would hold until morning," Boo said.

"How's that, Mr. Peterson?"

"Charlie, you can call me Beau or Boo, if you're more comfortable with that. I used some of that chain link fence that I took from the hardware store and attached it to the bottom of a few of the school buses. All we have to do is drive them in front of the entrances."

"Do you really think we need that?"

"I don't rightly know, to be honest with you. Sure wouldn't hurt having them blocked off, just in case," Boo replied.

Charlie shook his head not wanting to believe any of this was real. "I guess you're right, Mr. Peterson--I mean, Beau."

"There is one other thing that we need to talk about, Charlie. I know you have had a lot placed on your plate today...but this can't be overlooked."

"Sure, Beau, let's have it then," Charlie replied.

"It's like this, Charlie. I went over the amount of food and water they moved over here today. Water isn't a problem, because I can tap us into the river and pump water into the place for as long as we need. We can use the generator, or I can work something up using the wind or a bike." Boo paused to make sure Charlie was following. "Food, now that's another matter entirely. You have about thirty survivors so far, counting you, me, the Doctor and the group that came from the new school. You have enough food for about three days; unless we go on strict rations."

"There has to be more food in the houses," Charlie said out loud as he was thinking.

"That's my thinking exactly, Charlie! The whole world out there is just one big super store filled with supplies."

Charlie shook his head yes. "I will see if Doc has a truck that I can use to go shopping then."

"I think I will come along for the ride; we don't need a truck, we can use mine."

Charlie motioned for Boo to lead the way to his truck. Boo pointed over by the main stairs that rose up from Main Street into the school yard. "It's just down there, Charlie. I will meet you there in about five minutes." Charlie nodded his head and started off to Boo's truck.

He wasn't there very long when Boo appeared with Juan Martinez and his oldest boy in tow. "I thought maybe we should split the search up between two groups," Boo stated.

Charlie nodded his head in agreement. "Juan, Carlos, good to see you. Thanks for lending a hand," Charlie greeted them.

"Anything we can do to help you, Charlie. Anything at all," Juan replied.

"Thank you all the same, guys," Charlie said again, looking them over. "You look like you're going hunting for big game instead of canned beans."

"Charlie, we don't know what's in those houses," Boo stated, handing him a hand gun.

Charlie shook his head no several times as images from this morning flooded his head. Deep down, he knew that Boo was right; the world had moved on beyond the time of humans. Still, deep down inside of him, in a place where no creature or man could ever possibly find, there was his Annie. In that place there was no need for firearms or scrounging for food.

Charlie took the gun, "Let's get started then, gentlemen. Juan, you and your son start over on Front Street. Boo and I will start on Elm Street and meet you back here in the middle."

Charlie and Boo watched as Juan and Carlos rode off toward Front Street in the recently commandeered flatbed from the hardware store. Then they headed off toward Elm Street themselves with very little conversation until they reached their destination.

"Where do you want to start? Any preferences?" Boo asked Charlie.

"I think here on the corner is as good a place to start as any," Charlie replied.

"I will go up this side, Charlie, while you go up the other side. We can meet at the Preacher's house and do that one together." Charlie nodded his head and started toward the corner house on the other side of the street. It seemed odd to be going in other people's houses looking for things to take. He caught himself knocking on the front door and standing there, waiting for someone to answer; even had to stop himself from walking off when no one did.

Looking across the street he saw old Boo carrying out what looked like canned goods and coats. He gave a quick wave and Boo motioned for him to get a move on. Charlie frowned and reached down for the door handle. It was unlocked, to his surprise, so he went inside as if he had personally known the family that lived here. There was a pile of clothes in the front room, and all of the non-perishable food was neatly placed on the dining room table. In the kitchen it wasn't as neat; cabinets were all thrown open, and from what Charlie could see, they were bare. Charlie didn't bother with the double door refrigerator; nothing in there would be worth taking now.

A quick search upstairs offered little that could be used from Charlie's perspective, so he returned to the first floor and started carrying the food out to the truck. It looked like Boo was a few houses further down the street than he was, and the back of the truck bore the fruits of his labor. Charlie had hoped that he would live as long as Boo, and he also hoped that he had Boo's energy level when he got to that age. With Annie gone Charlie wasn't certain whether to think like that or not anymore.

Most of the houses didn't have a lot to offer, at least with respect to what they needed in the immediate future.

Boo had actually finished his side of the street and come over to take the next house after the one Charlie was in. They leap frogged each other until they reached the Preacher's house.

At the front door, Boo started giving Charlie hand signals. Charlie really had no clue as to what they meant. Boo, exhausted by Charlie's lack of action, kicked the front door in and entered the foyer. Charlie pointed his gun toward the back hall, where he heard a scratching sound. It reminded him of the scratching a puppy would make on the door to get back inside after being let out. Only this was slow and constant, without pause, more like a machine. The farther into the hall Charlie went, the louder the scratching became. Fixated on the scratching, Charlie was ignoring the doorways he passed. Just beyond the third door Charlie heard what sounded like an explosion, followed by a crushing weight falling upon him. The back of his head smacked the floor, sending white sparks off behind his eye. By reflex, he squeezed the trigger, discharging his gun. The weight stilled its movement.

Slowly the weight was lifted off of him, and he could see Boo's face near to his. Boo's lips were moving rapidly, but Charlie couldn't hear any words. All he could hear was a loud ringing that filled his head. Boo pulled him to his feet and pressed him against the wall, forcing the gun back into Charlie's shaking hand. On the floor lay what could have been the preacher's wife, possibly one of his daughters. At least that was what Charlie thought; he couldn't really tell from the bits of grotesque face remaining.

Boo motioned for Charlie to stay and made his way to the door at the end of the hall. Charlie couldn't hear the scratching anymore over the ringing. At that moment, for the first time in his life, Charlie knew what it meant to trust another with his life. An eighty-six year old man with a world war two era M1 Garand held Charlie's life in his ancient, shaky hands.

At the door Boo stopped, turned around, and pointed at Charlie, then at his own eyes, and finally, at the door. Charlie drew a deep breath and nodded yes. When Charlie raised the gun up and pointed it at the door, Boo shook his head and held up his open hand. One by one he bent a finger closed to his palm, counting down to when he would go in. Charlie tensed with fear as the second finger closed, then the last one. With a swift kick, Boo knocked the door off of its hinges, inward into the room. Charlie nearly squeezed off a round as it landed on the floor and the dust rose from beneath it. Like a man of thirty, Boo charged in the room never leaving Charlie's sight.

Charlie saw the defensive stance Boo took; then Boo lowered the M1 to his side and made a 'calm down' gesture with his free hand. Turning to Charlie, he repeated the gesture letting Charlie know it was ok. Stumbling forward, Charlie entered behind Boo and immediately saw the woman cowering in the corner. He wasn't sure of her name, but he knew that she had been an assistant to the Preacher for a few years. He felt guilty that he couldn't remember her name. Boo helped her to her feet and looked her over. There wasn't much left to her finger nails, from the looks of it she had been scratching on the door.

Charlie was starting to be able to hear again, as the ringing in his head died down. The woman said she was ok and asked if they could help her get out of there. Boo assured her and walked her past Charlie, out to the truck.

Charlie headed back up the hall pausing at every doorway and checking every room, before stopping when he found the kitchen. The refrigerator door was wide open; the smell of the rotten food was horrible. Pushing it shut, Charlie started going through the cabinets, but found only a can of condensed milk. Shaking his head, he wondered how many ran out of food. A moment of sadness overcame him as he started thinking about the preacher's family; what had gone through their minds when they first realized that there wasn't any food left. A rapid firing of shots from outside brought Charlie back to the moment.

"You Ok?" Charlie yelled on the way out the front door, startling Boo.

"We're good out here. That sounded like it came from the other side of town," Boo replied.

"Let's go check it out. Juan and his boy may have run into something like we did!"

Once inside of the truck, Boo tossed an old towel that he had pulled from behind the seat, over to Charlie. "Rip this up and wrap it around her fingers."

Catching the towel, Charlie saw that it was covered in oil or grease of some kind. He tossed it out the window. Reaching down to the bottom of his t-shirt, Charlie ripped off a big patch. Wrapping her hands the best he could, he looked over at Boo, "I don't know if they are infected, but I am fairly certain they would be if I used that dirty old towel."

"Point taken! Drop her off at the school, or go look for Juan, bringing her with?" Boo asked.

"No time. Bring her with."

"Hold on, then," Boo stepped down on the petal, hard, causing the truck to lurch forward.

They found the flatbed parked mid-way down Front Street, in front of the Donaldson's house, loaded down with supplies. Boo eased the truck up along the curb, blocking the driveway. The stairs leading up to the wrap around porch were covered in blood and bits of human flesh. From the distance, Charlie couldn't tell if it was Juan or his son. It could have been both, he thought to himself.

"Charlie, I want you to hang back with the girl. Move over here behind the wheel and keep the motor running," Boo ordered as he exited the cab.

"I don't think you should go in by yourself," Charlie replied.

"Probably not. Still, there is no reason that I can see for both of us to die today," Boo said with a smile.

Charlie watched Boo go up the stairs, leaving his foot prints in the blood. He paused for a few minutes over a torso, studying it, and then moved into the house. There was no sign of Boo for a long time after that. Charlie climbed out of the truck and checked his gun. As he started around the front of the truck, the first of five shots rang out. The shots were followed by Boo flying out of the back door backward, landing on top of the torso. A large creature came thru the door, cautiously at first, and then advanced on Boo with haste. Like Annie, this creature moved quickly and with purpose; not clumsily like the others.

Charlie raised the gun and fired, nicking the porch pillar with the first shot. The creature stopped and eyed Charlie for a brief second. Charlie recognized it as Ted Donaldson. Ted had made Charlie's life miserable growing up, and it looked like he was going to repeat it as a zombie. Charlie raised the gun again and held his breath while the monstrous Ted passed Boo on his way toward Charlie.

Steady, Charlie thought to himself as the space between them decreased. *Steady now.* He then fired, striking the Ted in the chest. It knocked him back a few feet, but didn't stop him. Charlie's next shot found its mark between the eyes, and down Ted, or what was left of him, went.

"Boo, you ok?"

Boo started coughing like he was fighting for breath, then settled down, "I am alive, if that is what you're asking. I thought I told you to stay in the truck, Charlie!"

"Lucky for you, I don't follow orders very well."

****

CHAPTER 8

Only a few hours after they had departed the bunker darkness was already settling over them and the snow fall was beginning to slow. Aunt Zoe, as the group had come to call her, had taken charge back at the barn and assigned vehicles to everyone. She seemed to have a logical sense of who should ride where. Zoe, Taquisha, Pam and the children were all in the RV, with Roy and Joey alternating turns driving. Lori, Virginia and the lads were in the truck leading the way. The rest were in the bus.

They weren't moving as fast as Lori would have liked, but they were making decent progress. Looking for a good spot to stop until morning, Lori noticed what looked like a small fire on the horizon. It seemed to be a few miles away, but it was hard to tell out in the middle of nowhere. The only way to judge the distance was by the occasional tree lines in between farm fields.

The closer they got to the fire, the more it looked like a small campfire. Then, the hulking back of a screen became visible, followed by a sign that read "Toby's Drive-in". Lori slowly brought the truck to a stop, and ordered Virginia to stay there and keep an eye out.

Jogging back to the RV door, Lori opened the door and went inside.

"Looks like there is a campfire over there behind the drive-in screen. I saw it a few miles back, but wasn't sure what it was until now."

"Think we should check it out?" Joey asked.

"Of course you should check it out!" Zoe stated. "There could be more survivors out there needing help."

Joey started to answer, "Aunt Zoe, what if…"

"No, she is right. We need to go in and take a look," Lori said, cutting Joey off.

Jermaine was standing at the open door, having come up to see why they were stopped. "I agree. Could be people, or something we could use."

"Jermaine, could you get Al and meet me by the truck, please?" Lori asked. "Joey, you and Roy come too. We will put

113

the dogs in here to keep everyone else safe while we are gone."

At the truck, Lori didn't wait for anyone to talk, starting into her plan for entering the drive-in. "Virginia, you put the dogs into the RV to keep the kids safe while we're out, and then climb up on top of the cab of the truck. Keep an eye out for anything that looks like a herd moving in on us."

Virginia shook her head yes and took the lads over to the RV. When she returned, she had Taquisha with her.

"The rest of us will go in through the exit, since it is right here by us. Once we can see what is there, we will split into groups and search through whatever we find."

Lori turned to Taquisha, "Are you sure you're up to this?"

Taquisha shook her head yes, and Jermaine patted her on the back. "That's my baby!"

They moved up near the exit, looking more like a group of kids heading into the school yard than a search party. No one said anything as the fear of the unknown began to grow. Just as they reached the drive-in screen, Lori looked back at Virginia who waved that she was ok.

In the drive-in parking lot there were rows of campers and trucks parked just short of the inclines that the cars used to raise their nose skyward towards the screen.

"There is more here than I thought would be," Lori stated.

"Yea, looks like there are a few fires burning towards the concession stand," Al offered.

Taquisha pointed a little further down the exit way at the ground. "Look over there, at the snow."

Following her finger, Lori could see that the snow about twenty yards down had been trampled flat to the gravel underneath. Whatever had been passing through there passed through in large numbers, and recently. "Can anyone see what is behind that tree line?" Lori asked.

"It's too dark. Do you want me to go look?" Joey asked.

Lori thought for a few minutes and decided against it. She wanted everyone to get back to the vehicles as fast as they could. "No, we should concentrate on the campers and the concession stand." She looked around at the different faces for their opinions. Handing Roy a flare gun retrieved from behind the truck's seat, Lori looked into his eyes, "Roy, can you stay here and watch that area? If anything moves from there just shoot the flare into the sky."

Roy nodded his head yes and took the gun from her. If Roy was honest with everyone there, he would have told them that he didn't want to leave the RV in the first place. It was beyond him as to why they were even stopping.

"Joey and Al, you take the first three rows of campers. Jermaine and Taquisha, if you could take the next three, please."

"Who's going with you?" Al asked

"I am going to make my way to the fire by the concession stand, then make my way toward you guys."

"I'm not sure it is a good idea for any of us to be alone," Jermaine stated.

"No issues leaving me here with a flare gun?" Roy asked.

Jermaine mock punched him in the arm. "Big man like you? No troubles at all."

"We should get moving. Faster we do this, the faster we are on the road again," Lori said, heading toward the concession stand. Behind her she could hear the others moving off as well.

There didn't seem, at first, to be any signs of people. It was as though they had just walked away from their portable shelters. Maybe that was why the snow was all trampled over there on the side of the lot, Lori thought. Deep down she knew what that trampled snow had meant. She hoped that they were far enough behind the herd so as to not have to deal with them in the dark.

The farther she moved, the stronger the scent filled her nose. *They're here alright. The question is, where?* Just beyond a beat up old Airstream trailer, Lori smelled something different. It had a sweet smell, like candy or cake. It was coming from the concession stand just ahead of her to the left. Inside there were sounds of something moving around so Lori loaded an arrow and pulled the door open quickly, slamming it against the outside wall. Twenty faces lit by candle light stared blankly back, unsettling her for a moment. The smell wasn't zombie at all, just more of that sweet aroma filling the room.

117

Jermaine and Taquisha were searching through the third or fourth camper when a shuffling sound caught Jermaine's attention. He motioned to Taquisha to stop rummaging through the cabinets for a second, so he could concentrate.

"Did you hear anything that sounded like a flare going off?" He asked Taquisha.

Shaking her head no, Taquisha went back to looking for anything she thought they could use.

"Baby, be still for a few seconds. Something is outside of the camper," Jermaine whispered.

Taquisha gave Jermaine her best exasperated look as she turned and left the camper. Having grown increasingly used to that reaction, Jermaine strained to hear if the shuffling was still present. It had stopped for the moment and that was pleasing until Taquisha screamed. Jermaine rushed to her side with ax raised, at the ready. There was one creature, stopped as if it was as surprised at the sight of them, as they were of it.

"Back up slowly, baby, and get behind me," Jermaine ordered as he moved slowly forward. The creature didn't make any attempts to move forward, or to flee. Raising the ax higher, Jermaine brought it down with a whooshing sound, using all of the might he had. The ax landed squarely above the creature's right eye, crushing into the skull. The creature fell to the ground with a thud; the ax still embedded in it's skull. Jermaine stepped on the head and pulled the ax free, noticing that there were more coming from around the front of the camper. Grabbing Taquisha, he pulled her toward the back where they found even more coming toward them.

"Come on, baby! Head towards the far end! You run as fast as you can, and don't look back! You hear me, Taquisha?"

Nodding her head, Taquisha took off as fast as she could. At the far end of the drive-in she could barely make out a sign that said "EXIT" in glowing white letters.

Al heard the scream and motioned for Joey to drop what he was carrying, and get going. Joey pointed to the growing herd around them and then to a narrow piece of open space between two of the campers. Al nodded yes, and motioned for Joey to go. In between the campers was tight and confined. Al knew if they had to fight in there the weapons that they had brought would be next to useless. Uncertain they would be able to get out alive, Al began praying for help. On the other end, the creatures were more focused on something that Al and Joey couldn't make out, just beyond what they could see. Regardless, it was the break Al had prayed for. To him, it was nothing less than a miracle.

"This way, Joey," Al said out loud, alerting the creatures to their presence. The creatures moved faster than Al had ever seen before, enveloping them. Their hands were all over his body as he fought to free himself. Reaching into his pocket for the revolver and forcing it free against the mass pressing in against him, Al began firing off shots into anything until it seemed that a little room was opening up to move. This herd had come upon them so rapidly it was difficult to keep his wits about him. With a little more room to work with Al's shots were finding their mark in the heads of the creatures. Each shot sent exploding decaying matter all over him, and what he thought was Joey.

"Joey, where are you, son?" Al screamed out as the last of the rounds from the gun fired off. Al had always been a firm believer in the Almighty, and in angels. If asked, Al would say that angels came in all colors and sizes. Now, he couldn't say if they really had wings and all of that, but he could tell that he believed that the almighty would send an angel when needed most. Before him now was an angel if he had ever seen one; a six foot-plus, nearly two hundred and fifty pound, angel wielding an ax as if it was Gabriel's sword.

Jermaine had come toward the sound of the gun fire and threw himself into the fight with little to no regard for his own safety. When he got close enough to Al, Jermaine pointed toward Joey, lying on the ground in a pool of blood and, "Get your boy and go toward the exit. Taquisha should be there with that little girl and the dogs, I hope."

Al picked up his bloody son, relieved to see that he was still alive, and helped Joey towards the exit sign. Behind him, Al could hear Jermaine gasping for breath and the swoosh of the ax, followed by a thick thud as it landed on its mark.

"Quick! Close the door before they get here!" a voice shouted at Lori.

"It isn't safe to stay here. You can come with me and get out of this place, or you can stay here and die!" Lori yelled into the room.

"This is the only place that they can't get into. You're safe here," the voice replied, sounding agitated with the door remaining open.

"I have a bus that can carry all of you with us, but you need to leave now!"

About ten people moved toward Lori, causing her to raise the crossbow up into a defensive position.

"We will go with you," a voice said.

"Follow me, and stay close then. We are going to go out the exit on the far side. If you get separated, keep going that way and look for the bus on the road."

The zombies were not heading toward the concession stand as Lori had thought. They were swarming around the first few aisles in the center. For them, it would be an easy run to the exit. She could smell the zombies on the wind blowing across the lot. It had troubled her earlier that she could smell them, but she was grateful now. It made it easier to move the new members of her party.

Arriving at the exit, Lori was relieved to see everyone there anxiously waiting. Joey looked badly hurt, but everyone else looked like they were in good shape despite their ordeal.

"We need to get to the bus," Lori stated as she moved past them. Jermaine took Joey from Al, picking him up as if he were a rag doll.

"They are coming too," a little boy said to Lori, pointing towards the entrance.

Lori looked back at a small group emerging from the exit. They moved quicker than the herd, but not by much. After the last of the new members were loaded onto the bus Joey was loaded into RV so that Zoe could do what she could for her great nephew. It would be Zoe who would have the final say in the matter. Roy climbed into the RV to be greeted by quizzical looks.

"I didn't hear or see the flare, man!" Jermaine said as he grabbed Roy by the throat.

"Not now! We have to get moving," Lori said as she left the RV, slamming shut the door.

"You and I are going to have a long talk when we stop, bro," Jermaine dropped Roy to the floor of the RV, leaving his gasping to catch his breath.

*****

Doc had watched the two trucks head off to opposite ends of the town from the school's roof before turning his attention back to the activity going on inside. Doc checked in on the progress of the rooms on the second floor, then moved on to the first floor. Everyone was pulling together nicely with the job of making the old school into a home. For as hard as the survivors were working, Doc knew that something was missing. Yes, they were doing what was asked of them, and doing it well; no one could complain. What was missing was a spark of life, he thought. The major difference right now, between them and the zombies, was that they could bleed and think clearly. If they were going to succeed and rebuild some kind of civilized existence Doc knew that they would have to find a way to return that spark of life.

It was then that the unmistakable smell of coffee had overcome his senses. Doc followed his nose down to the gymnasium/cafeteria where he found a rather large man and somewhat smaller woman putting the supplies away. Doc edged his way over to the large coffee urn, looking for anything that would serve as a cup.

"Cups are over there, below the counter," the woman stated, not looking so small now that he was up close. Perhaps it was that the man was so large that he made Doc feel extra small himself.

"Help yourself," she added.

"Don't mind if I do," Doc replied, reaching over the counter and fumbling around for a cup. Finding one, he held it under the spigot and reveled in the indulgent aroma of fresh coffee.

"Found three boxes of coffee earlier; I thought maybe people would like a cup after working so hard all day," she added.

Doc took a sip, "Mmmm-ummm. That is a good cup of coffee, Miss...?"

"Tressa Harris is my name, and that over there is my uncle, Todd," she replied motioning at the large man. "And you are the legendary Doctor Stewart, I believe?"

"You would be correct, Tressa. It is a pleasure to meet both of you and drink your coffee."

Doc thought for a few minutes about the two floors he had just passed through above. This was the spark he was looking for. "Did someone ask you to do this?" Doc asked.

Tressa shook her head no, "We didn't know that we had to get permission to put supplies up. Is there someone that we should have cleared it with first?"

"Heavens, no! I wish I knew how to get more people to be like you two."

The large man stopped what he was doing and walked over to Doc, stopping only when he was hovering over him.

"Mister, maybe they don't understand that they will get a surprise for helping out. Tressa says if I work hard I will get a surprise when we are all done. Right, Tressa?"

"Yes, Todd. Do you remember what the surprise is going to be?"

The large man screwed his face deep in thought staring at the ceiling as if the answer would magically appear before him.

126

"What is one of your favorite things to have on a cold winter's day like this, Todd?" She asked him.

The answer was there and Doc could see, in his face, that the man had found it. Then with very little warning, he started jumping up and down while twirling around in circles yelling, "Hot coco with tiny marshmallows in it! Hot coco with tiny marshmallows in it!"

Tressa patted him on the back in an attempt to settle him back down, "Ok, Todd. If you want that hot coco, you need to get back to work. Those boxes aren't going to move themselves are they?"

"They better not Tressa. I am going to move them all and get my hot chocolate!" As quick as he had moved in on Doc, he had moved back to the boxes.

Maybe it was the puzzled look on Doc's face, maybe it was the way he hadn't said anything after Todd came over by him. Whatever it was, Tressa felt she needed to speak up now before they found themselves, once again, on the outside looking in.

"My uncle is a very special soul. He is a five-year-old trapped in a grown man's body."

127

"A very, very large man's body," Doc replied shaking his head.

"Yes sir, he is large and strong as an ox. He doesn't know that we are not stronger than he is. In Todd's mind we are the larger and stronger ones." Letting out a long, deep sigh she continued, "His whole life he has been picked on, made fun of, and bullied because of his size. Let me tell you this before you make your mind up about us, Doctor! That large mountain of a man that you're deciding if you need to fear, watched his own parents--my grandparents--get ripped apart by the zombie while he cowered and cried for someone to help them. THAT is what to be afraid of, not my uncle!"

Doc took a step back and placed his coffee cup down. "I would like to have ten more of him, little lady. If you were thinking that I was about to put you out of here then you are wrong." Doc could see the relief in the young woman's face. "In fact, how would you like to be in charge of the kitchen for now?"

Tressa smiled and replied, "I think I would like that, for now."

"Well then, I guess that is settled. Now we need to figure out how to get the others to pitch in on their own."

Tressa thought for a few minutes then added, "That should be simple, assign them daily chores to do. It works wonders with Todd; makes him feel like he is part of a team.

Doc thought a few minutes and liked the idea. They would assign chores out to every survivor here. They would be made responsible for pulling their weight from this point on.

****

CHAPTER 9

Jermaine opened the RV door and headed straight for the bus where he thought he would be able to calm himself down. Anyplace but where Roy was would be good enough for now.

"Virginia!" Al called out as the girls left the RV. Virginia turned and faced him, wondering what he could need from her.

"Do you think you could ride in the RV with Zoe, and let me ride with Lori for a little while?"

Virginia didn't want to be in the RV, she liked riding in the truck with Lori and was about to say so when, from behind her, Lori answered for her. "Of course she will, Al! And she will take the dogs with her."

Turning and giving Lori a questioning look while rolling her eyes, she turned back to Al, "For you and Zoe, the lads and I will ride in the RV."

"If the roads don't get any worse we should be in Rivers Crossing by the morning," Lori stated.

"A lot can happen between now and the morning," Virginia said as she motioned for the lads to follow her back into the RV. From inside she watched Al and Lori climb into the truck. A few minutes later she could feel the balding tires of the old RV slipping through the snow in an effort to keep up with the convoy. The RV was as quiet as a church during Sunday mass, with the exception of Zoe's calming words to Joey. Now and then she would come forward to get more towels or rags in her efforts to stem the bleeding. Zeus was keeping a close eye on her and Joey from a vantage point that forced Zoe to climb over him with every trip forward. She never complained or asked him to move. Occasionally she would reach down and pat him on the head in passing.

After several trips, Zoe motioned for Roy to let her sit next to Virginia. He begrudgingly moved over, and in his own way gave Virginia a hateful look. Zoe took one of Virginia's hands and said to her, "Do you know why I asked Al to ask you to ride with me, child?"

At that moment Virginia knew why she was in the RV with amazing clarity. Zoe didn't think that Joey was going to make it. More than that, Zoe must have thought that Joey was going to turn.

131

"When the time comes, you want me to do what needs to be done," Virginia replied.

The first signs of tears were starting to show in Zoe's eyes as she reached over and fully embraced Virginia. "I am not asking you to do it, child. I am asking you to do it if, when the time comes, I can't."

Zoe let let Virginia go and returned back to where Joey was laying; leaving Virginia to think about what she had said.

"You really think you're something, don't you?" Roy said, more as a statement than a question. Virginia slid over to him real close. Close enough that Taquisha and Pam had noticed. It was closer than even Pam had been to Roy in a long time.

With her lips nearly touching Roy's face, Virginia said, "I saw what you did tonight from up on top of the bus. I know exactly what you did, and that you stood there, in front of that woman, and her father, and told a bunch of lies."

Roy made a motion to move away from her when Perseus let out a low menacing growl, causing him to still. Virginia raised a finger to his lips and pressed it against him. "If you give me any reason, anything at all, I will let those dogs rip your throat out and feed what is left of you to the Zombies. Perhaps, before I put poor Joey out of his misery, I will let him eat you. Wouldn't that be justice?"

Roy froze in place, feeling like he might pee his pants if Virginia made the slightest move on him. Instead Virginia slid back to the place where she had been sitting. Pam wanted to say something, but the words didn't come to her. Pam really wanted to know what the girl had said, but at the same time she just wanted the odd, little kid as far from her as possible.

"You know this has all been foretold in the bible," Taquisha stated as she closed her eyes. "The Lord took home all of the good people, and left the evil ones to deal with the devil's minions."

There wasn't a chance to reply to Taquisha; Zoe came out and motioned for Virginia to come to the back of the RV. Rising slowly, Virginia pulled an arrow out of her quiver and made the short walk back to join Zoe, who was looking down on Joey. His eyes were black, and the tone of his skin had begun to turn gray. He looked nothing at all like Lori had on the night Virginia snuck onto the bus to say good bye.

Knowing why she was summoned to the back, and being able to do it now that she was back there, were two different things. Yes, Virginia could kill a zombie without thinking twice, or even reflecting on it afterward. This was Joey. Someone she knew--and had in some small way--even kind of liked. Looking down on him now, Virginia saw the transformation taking place, but she also saw Joey.

"Are you positive that this is what you want?" Virginia asked Zoe.

"It's not what I want, child. It's what needs to be done before he puts everyone in the RV in danger."

Virginia raised the arrow up high as Joey's dead eyes stared up at her. For an instant she thought there were signs of Joey looking at her, pleading with her for life. Then the low guttural growl rumbled deep in his throat.

The arrow came down with blinding speed into the center of his eye. Pulling it out, Virginia sank it deep into the other eye with a twisting motion. There was no more movement that she could see or feel. Joey had been a good friend; now she had ended him at Zoe's request. It wasn't fair that someone as good as Joey had to go this way while a piece of shit like Roy was still alive.

Turning to exact justice for Joey from Roy's flesh, Virginia ran smack into Zoe who threw her arms around her. "I am sorry you had to do that for me, child. I just couldn't."

"I can make this right."

Zoe pushed Virginia back so as to see her face and look into her eyes. "Make what right, Virginia?"

"I can make Roy pay for what he did," Virginia replied.

Zoe pulled her into another deep hug, stroking her hair and said softly, "Only God can make this right, child. He will settle all things when each of us meets him."

Virginia pulled back in shock. *How could Zoe think that there is still a God, if there ever had been one in the first place? That man sat out there alive and smug, because he was a coward that ran before warning the others. They were lucky that only one had died because of him, and not the whole group!* Virginia thought.

"Look at me, Virginia!" Zoe ordered in that Aunt Zoe way that demanded respect

135

and compliance. "We will give that man out there a chance to prove himself. We will give him another chance, because it is the Christian thing to do. We will give him another chance, because it is what *I* want to do!"

"But he…"

"He did nothing worse than be afraid! I am afraid nearly all of the time, child! He did not kill my nephew; those creatures did."

In Virginia's world, everything was cut and dry; black and white. Zombies were bad so you killed them, with the same amount of thought as you would when stepping on a cockroach. You killed them or they ate you; it was as simple as that. Now she was being asked to look for a higher reason to not kill someone who deep down she knew would bring harm, who would place the group in danger. That didn't work in Virginia's world.

Zoe could see the confusion in Virginia's face, "Now, if someone with two large dogs wanted to keep an eye on him-- just to make sure that there was no more shenanigans--I believe the good Lord wouldn't have a problem with that, and neither would I."

Virginia smiled, "I will signal the others that we need to stop to take care of Joey."

"Thank you, child. You do that," Zoe said, letting her pass.

Once the signal was passed on from the RV to the bus, and finally to Lori, the group once again came to a stop. There was no question in anyone's mind as to why they were stopping. There was a little bit of concern about how safe it would be, but everyone understood why. Lori and Al walked the area looking for signs of the dead moving near. Lori ventured a little further from the vehicles than Al did, but she thought that was ok. It had been a long and painful day for Al.

"I don't think we can bury him here, or that we should even try," Al said to Lori.

"We can keep moving until we find a better place, Al. It's up to you."

"No, he is my son and I don't think I want to ride with him since the change started, so I am sure no one else does either," Al replied.

Zoe came towards them from the RV, moving slowly through the snow. "Is this the best we can find, Albert?"

Al rolled his eyes while his face was looking away from her. "The ground is frozen, Aunt Zoe, and a little ways down the hill you can see the zombies are moving. I don't know how much time we will have here."

"Surely you are not planning on leaving my nephew, your son, lying out here in the snow?"

"It may be best to burn the body, Zoe," Lori added. "Just to be safe."

"I would like to say a few words over him before we do that," Zoe pleaded.

Lori could feel the zombies off in the darkness, even if she couldn't quite see them right now. It wasn't really a feeling; she knew they were there. Just like she knew that Zoe and Al were standing right in front of her.

"Whatever you want to do, Zoe. Let's just do it quickly, if we can."

138

Virginia watched from off to the side as firewood was hauled from the back of the truck to make a bed for Joey to lay on. There wasn't much conversation as Zoe walked up to her great nephew and said a few prayers. A few times her voice broke up, but she continued to the end. Al didn't have the strength to say anything, but she could see what he was thinking in his eyes. Silently, he walked back and lit a quickly fashioned torch, then turned back to his son. "God, please take my son into your loving arms," Al said as he touched the torch to the gas soaked firewood. With a blaze, Joey was engulfed in flames and it was all over. Everyone silently turned back toward the vehicles.

Taquisha watched the small crowd retreat from the funeral pyre and shook her head.

"Don't you all see the truth of it all?" she screamed into the night.

"Baby, let's get back into the bus and talk about it," Jermaine pleaded with her.

"Talk? There is nothing for us to talk about! We all know the truth, and it is time to accept it!"

From behind them, the zombies were making their way towards the group, following Taquisha's voice. "Look, honey. We need to get moving now. Can we talk about this later?" Jermaine continued.

******

CHAPTER 10

"Hey, Doc. Are you down there?" a voice yelled down the stairs. Doc swung around from the lunch counter, and walked over to the bottom of the wide, old stairway.

"I'm here," he replied, squinting his eyes to see who it was, then recognizing the voice had belonged to Charlie. He smiled up at him. "Was this morning successful?"

Charlie started down the stairs to meet him as Doc started up the stairs.

"We lost Juan and his son. They must have walked in on a bunch of creatures on the last house of the street. There wasn't a whole lot of them left. Boo and I found the church secretary hiding in a closet at the preacher's house. I can honestly tell you that if it wasn't for Boo, I would have ended up like Juan. He must have been hell on wheels thirty or forty years ago!"

"Charlie, I am so sorry to hear about Juan and his boy," Doc stated with a rare tear running down his cheek. Since moving all of the survivors to the old school, Doc had appointed himself as the caretaker of all who resided here. It was him that woke

141

every morning and made the rounds to check on them. He cleaned up after them, nursed them back to health when they needed it, and healed them when he could. Juan had been a great help to him in keeping the place going, and as far as he could tell, Juan was one of the few that Beau trusted to touch the boiler.

"What kind of shape is the secretary in? Wasn't her name Donna?" Doc asked

Charlie shrugged his shoulders, because he really didn't know the woman's name. Annie had always wanted to go to church, but had never really pushed the subject very far. Mostly, she went on her own and left Charlie to do as he pleased. Deep down, Charlie knew that it wouldn't have hurt him to give in to her and regretted a little not going with her.

Doc started up the stairs without another word until reaching the top, "Where did Beau take her?"

"I think he's headed over to the nurse's office, or--I mean--your office," he replied with a smile. Doc smiled back at their inside joke. That joke was from a bygone time that existed only in their memories; Sunday morning coffee meetings.

142

He would miss those. Doc led the way toward the nurses' office.

They found Boo going over his field dressing of the secretary's wounds. Stepping next to him, Doc took over from there, "What are your thoughts?"

"Oh, I think she will survive well enough," Boo replied, stepping out of Doc's way.

Doc took a long look at the avulsions on each of her finger tips, mumbled to himself a few times, and then led the woman over to the sink.

"This may sting a little, but only for a few minutes," Doc explained to her, looking deeply into her eyes for any sign that she understood what he was saying. Seeing nothing, he took her left hand first and held it under the cold water. With no signs of any discomfort, he added in the kitchen soap that was sitting next to the faucet. Then Doc noticed a slight attempt to pull back, followed by a barely audible wince. "So you are in there someplace," Doc stated as he quickly moved on to her right hand. Once he felt they were cleaned out enough to meet his personal standards, he pulled a clean towel from the drawer and lightly dabbed them dry. "Charlie, in that cabinet behind you, there is some gauze and a bottle of antiseptic ointment. Be a good fellow and grab them for me, will you?"

Charlie retrieved the items and handed them to Doc. It was amazing to watch Doc in his element, taking care of people. There was no way that Charlie could deal with this day in and day out. This was what Doc did for over thirty years or more of his life.

"OK, my dear. Why don't you lie down over here and rest awhile, and we will find you a bed of your own," Doc stated as he led her to one of the old nurse's beds for sick students. Once she was safely in the bed and covered up with an old blanket that Doc had found, he gave her a Vicodin to help with any pain she might be feeling. Since she could not, or would not, tell the pain level she was feeling, Doc only gave her one. He also knew needed to save as many as he could for more serious injuries that would come up down the line.

"Well, let's get out of here and let the young lady rest. Later on I will ask Tressa to make her something light to eat, like broth, if we have any," Doc said, ushering them out of the room into the hall. Once there Charlie asked, "Tressa?"

"While you boys were out, a few survivors came in from the east."

"How many?" Boo asked looking concerned

"I think about fifteen, maybe twenty," Doc replied.

This brought Boo to a dead stop, shaking his head no. "Doc, you need to be careful about who you let in here until they are checked out! How in the hell did they even know we were here?"

"Not sure, Beau. You could ask any of them yourself if you really feel we need to know that type of information."

Boo's face was turning beet red as he tried to control himself, feeling his temper boil to the top. "Yes Sir! We do need to know that info from everyone that comes in; we need to know where they came from as well! There are people out there that were not so nice when the world was intact... do you really think that they have ceased to exist now? Do you honestly believe that if they were evil then, that all of this has changed that?"

Doc was flabbergasted. No one had ever spoken to him like this in all of his years. "Follow me, please," Boo stated more as an order than a question. "I want you to get a good look at something. Maybe then you can get a handle on the predicament that we now live in!"

*****

Taquisha turned her back to Jermaine and raised her hands towards the sky to pray. Long ago he had learned not to interrupt her during prayer. Taquisha had put up with all of his screw ups in life with hardly a word that held him accountable or discouraged him from trying to do better the next time. No matter what, she had stuck by his side when others had called for her to dump him and move on in hopes of finding a more conventional man that went to work every day. Instead, she had stuck by his side while he went in and out of jail. The one thing she did not tolerate, was any interference with her relationship with God. Jermaine knew better and did not interfere and that is why they stayed together; at least that was why he thought they did. Jermaine knew that she would not move until she was either done, or there were zombies nearly on top of her. Jermaine turned to go wait by the RV door. He could keep a fairly good eye on things from there and react accordingly if he needed to. This gave Taquisha the space she would need, and him some peace of mind.

"Should I send the dogs out there to watch over Taquisha?" Virginia asked when he reached the door.

Jermaine chuckled a little and then replied, "Not unless you want to make the ride ahead that much more unbearable."

"I didn't think that was possible to do," Virginia replied with a slight smile.

"Oh trust me with Taq, all things are possible in that area."

They both laughed for a few seconds, as they watched her, illuminated by the flames of Joey's funeral pyre.

Then the oddest thing happened in front of them and neither was prepared to act with the speed to stop it. Taquisha, with her arms still raised, screamed out, "Forgive me, father, for I have sinned against you!" then started sprinting toward where the zombies were gathering, just behind the slight drainage ditch. They were barely visible without looking hard for the movements of

147

shadows in the darkness. Taquisha's scream brought them out of the shadows and into the light; both Jermaine and Virginia could see that it was a decent sized herd now.

Before either of them could react Taquisha was in the center of the herd, surrounded, with no way out, still screaming to the lord. The last thing Jermain heard as he sprinted toward his wife was, "If God wills it!" ...then nothing. Not even a cry for help.

Reaching the periphery of the herd, Jermaine smashed his fist through the skull of the first zombie. The partially decomposed facial bones crushed inward beneath the force of his strike and collapsed around his hand. It made a suction sound as he pulled his fist back out of the cranium, coated in what had once been brain tissue. He did the same on another as the herd now swallowed him, much the same way it had Taquisha. Jermain didn't know or care about what was happening around him. He was ready to fight his way to Taquisha and pull her out at all costs. Even if the cost to save his wife was paying with his own life; Jermaine would see it paid in full. There were no feelings of pain or fear in that moment, only a deep rage that boiled over. His large stature made it nearly impossible for the herd to pull him down like they had Taquisha. In no time he had fought his way to what had been his wife's body. There were so many zombies feasting on her that there was no way to tell what kind of shape she was in, or if she was even in one piece anymore. None of this mattered to Jermaine. He would reach the woman he loved and pull her from this unholy place. *Taquisha would want this*, he kept telling himself.

The first zombie he pulled off of her had a large piece of her intestines in its hands as he threw the creature off of her, knocking down several other zombies. The second had what Jermain had thought was her beautiful face. The very face that kept him going during each and every jail term he had spent back in the day. Seeing that beautiful face made his knees go weak with the realization that there was hardly anything left of Taquisha. The weight of the herd now pulling and ripping at his own flesh finally began to bear down on him, bringing him to the ground. Reaching out, he grabbed Taquisha's hand and held it in his. He would die holding her hand. Something ripped at the flesh on his back, causing a surge of pain to ripple throughout his body, and Jermaine thought it would all be over soon. Only the guttural growling noise from the zombies, and the hand of his wife in his own were clear in his mind. He failed to even notice that he was holding a hand attached to a disembodied arm wrenched from her body by the zombies.

A deeper, more vicious growl, brought him back to his senses; something more animal than monster. Rapidly the weight on his back disappeared. The herd retreated slightly, opening up a large circle around him, and a warm tongue licked the tears streaming down his face. Jermaine was looking at Perseus.

Circling around him, snarling with the look of a menacing, black killing machine, was Zeus; keeping the circle of zombies from closing back in on them. One... then two more zombies fell to the ground with arrows in the eyes. As he looked back up, Virginia was standing next to him. "I think we need to get going while Zeus has them held back! Follow Perseus toward the others!" she ordered Jermaine.

"Taquisha is..."

"She is dead, and there is nothing we can do about it. People die, Jermaine, and we that are living move on! If you ever loved her, then get up and run for the others!"

Jermaine pulled himself up off the ground and looked at the little girl beside him. *Not really a little girl*, he thought; more of an old soul trapped in a teenager's body. Too old of a soul for a person her age.

"We need to move!"

Jermaine ran for the RV as Perseus cleared a path, Zeus keeping pace behind them, maintaining the herd at a distance. What had taken seconds to get into seemed like it was taking a life time to get out of; only when he noticed the zombies on either side of him were falling to the ground did he begin to feel like this part of the ordeal was coming to an end. He was sure of it when he saw Lori and her bow firing arrows all around them as they came out of the herd into open space. At that point the real firepower opened up around them. The sound of all the guns going off was deafening, while music to his ears at the same time. A few minutes ago, Jermaine had accepted that it was his time to meet his maker and join Taquisha. Now he wanted nothing more than to be safely in one of the vehicles, moving as far from here as possible.

By the funeral pyre, a tug pulled on what was left of his coat sleeve, causing him to snap around with fists raised. It was Virginia, holding his sleeve with a funny look on her face.

"What is it?"

She pointed toward the funeral pyre and then toward Jermaine's right hand. He was still holding the severed arm that had belonged to Taquisha. The tears began to flow freely again as he looked at what was left of her.

"I don't think that Joey or Taquisha would mind this part of her sharing a final resting place with Joey," Virginia said as she patted his shoulder lightly with a warm caring look on her face. Jermaine was taken aback by this side of her; a side that he had not seen since joining them back at the old farm house. He thought for a few minutes, and said a quiet prayer to himself as best he could. Then, with a heavy heart, Jermaine walked up to the fire and laid the arm onto the pyre.

After a few minutes, Jermaine placed his hand on Virginia's back and said, "Thank you." They turned back on their way to the RV, where they were ushered inside.

From what Jermaine could remember before they had stopped here, they were as close as maybe four or five more hours from the next stop on the map Lori had showed him back at the farm house. It would be good to reach a safe place where he could mend his body, and his heart, without being cooped up with all these people. Most of them had grown on him, a few had not. As for the new ones from the drive in, well, he would have see how that all played out. The one thing that Jermaine knew for certain was that he would stay with this group and help out as much as he could. Deep down there was a part of him that wondered about Virginia and the dogs coming to his rescue. No one had ever put their life on the line to save his life before. Taquisha tried to save him spiritually, lord knew that she had tried. That was different. Virginia ran into that herd--and the dogs followed her—just to save him. This day would live in his memory for the rest of his days. The bravery of a young woman and her dogs had moved Jermaine in a way nothing in his old life ever had; a power larger and stronger than anything he had ever known.

******

CHAPTER 11

Boo led them up to the roof of the old school to a place he had taken to calling the 'Eagle's Nest' due to the unobstructed view it offered of the surrounding countryside. He stopped close to the three foot high wall that ran the entire way around the roof and pointed out towards the farms to the east of Rivers Crossing.

"Take a good look out there, boys, and tell me what you see," Boo ordered them. When no one answered, he prodded them on, "Go ahead now, don't be shy." After waiting for what felt like an eternity extending his finger out towards the nearest farm Boo stated, "That mass moving around out there could be confused with a prized herd of Holsteins!"

Charlie could finally see where Boo was going with this so he replied, "They're still a few miles off, Boo."

"Moving closer every day. We need to start planning things around here a little better if we are going to survive, fellas. This isn't a game, or a community center where survivors check in to be taken care of by the local Red Cross or FEMA. We are, for all

154

purposes, a city state like in ancient times; we need to start acting like one," Boo stated what he felt was an indisputable matter-of-fact.

Doc shook his head no a few times, "What if there is some part of the government left out there?"

"We can wait for the cavalry to arrive and save the day. Or we can plan on saving ourselves and still be around if, and when, the cavalry arrives. It would be a sad thing if we all perished holding on to the false hope that someone is coming to save us, Doc."

"I think I agree with Boo on this one, Doc. We haven't seen anything that has even looked like help for weeks," Charlie added.

Doc went into his deep thought process, a process that Charlie had seen a million times during discussion at the Sunday Morning coffee meetings. Those seemed to be a life time away now. Charlie knew when Doc went to that place and got that blank stare on his face you could bet the farm that he was going to come back with something so irrefutable that you had just wasted your time making the argument.

"Ok, I can see your point on the whole thing, Beau, but I am not saying that I agree with you one hundred percent. I think we should elect a city council and a Mayor as I have stated before."

"If you're going to do that, we should probably do it before any more outsiders show up. I like to think that, for now anyways, we would be governed by locals," Boo replied.

Doc smiled a little evil looking grin at the two men. "I can see your point completely. We will appoint the first council with people that we want on there so that we can point the city in the proper direction."

"That's fine by me. You go ahead and pick your council. Make yourself the Mayor while you're at it; but the first thing you need to do is create some kind of guard unit so we can watch over and protect what it is that we have here. Someone to man this post twenty four hours a day so that nothing can take us by surprise," Boo added.

Charlie was shocked at what he was hearing. They were deciding the fate of every survivor in Rivers Crossing without even including them in the process. This may have been how Boo did things, but it wasn't how the Doc he knew conducted business or his life.

"So we are setting up a dictatorship?" he asked.

"No, no! Not at all, Charlie! We will appoint the first council and Mayor so that we can create our own little Constitution, and ensure that no one in the future can become a dictator. If Beau here is correct, and I sincerely hope he is not, then we need to plan for a future without the life we knew before. One where everyone will have a chance at life, liberty, and some kind of pursuit of happiness. I was talking this morning with the woman in the cafeteria-- her name is Tressa--and I realized that there are only a few of us doing anything to keep the place going. We can't function that way."

"Everyone needs to pull their weight, or they need to try it on their own out there," Boo added nodding his head in agreement.

"I understand that, and I am not saying that I don't agree with both of you. Couldn't we just ask them to do more as part of the team?"

"We will, Charlie. We will post jobs on the bulletin board at the entrance after the council selects and offers the lead positions to people," Doc replied.

"I guess you didn't really need Boo to bring this up to you, Doc?" Charlie asked.

Doc walked over to the edge on the other side of the roof and looked off to the east for a few seconds, then he turned back towards Boo and Charlie. "I have been watching the creatures coming closer to Rivers Crossing as well, and watching how things are going down stairs. Most of the survivors down there are about as dead as the creatures are out there. They don't seem to have anything left to live for really. Like us, they have lost most of their loved ones. Like us, they don't believe deep down that there is anything left out there to come and save them. I said earlier that I was talking to Tressa and her uncle when Charlie came to get me. They had taken it upon themselves to unpack and put up supplies. They weren't just going through the motions because I asked them to do it. They were doing a job; feeling like they were part of the team even though they had only just come to Rivers Crossing this morning. We need that type of feeling to become contagious. We need people to wake up in the morning feeling like they are making a difference; like they are sharing in making this place a lasting home for all of us."

Charlie smiled at both of them, "Ok, I am onboard with your plot; you have convinced me. How do we get started?"

"Doc, you see the people more than Charlie and I do, and you have been working with the survivors. Who would you suggest for the first council?" Boo asked.

Doc looked up at that the sky, as if he thought the answer would be written somewhere among the clouds, "I think we should limit the council to six people, and the mayor would be the deciding vote if anything came down to a tie. I know she is not a local, but I would like that Tressa be a council member, along with you, Charlie, myself, Elisabeth Windsor and the church secretary."

"The church secretary? Really, Doc? She doesn't even speak as far as we know!" Charlie questioned. "And as far as I am concerned... I don't think that is something I would be very good at-or something that I want to do!"

"No, Charlie. Doc is right. For now, we need the three of us on that council to make sure things go in the right direction," Boo replied.

"Then I hope it is a short term. I have told you both more than once that come spring…"

"We know, Charlie. As soon as the weather breaks, you're finding a Harley and riding off into the sunset," Boo interrupted him. "You know, you might just decide to stay if things go as planned."

"You keep telling yourself that, Boo. Just remember that just because you keep saying it, doesn't mean that that's how it is going to happen!"

"I am just having fun with you, Charlie," Boo said clapping Charlie on the back.

"We can decide the term length when the full council meets," Doc stated. "I think we should try to do that today,; then announce tonight, in the cafeteria."

"I agree, the sooner we get this going, the better off we will be. In fact, if what is here of the new Rivers Crossing Council will agree, I am going to start picking people for the new guard unit," Boo replied.

"I think that is a good idea, Beau. Furthermore, I think we should appoint you to be a head of it," Doc replied.

"I would be honored," Boo replied. "Now if you two can set up the first council meeting; I am going to rustle up a few people that look like they can shoot straight."

"OK, let's meet back here around four o' clock then. Agreed?"

All agreed to return to the roof at four with the other three council members. No one knew if the church secretary would be able to join them, but Charlie suspected there was a reason that Doc had picked her. Maybe he was trying to make it look like the moral side of things would be selected. If you didn't have a preacher, you could at the very least have his secretary. That was the most sense Charlie could make of it at the moment; for now he decided to go with the flow.

*****

CHAPTER 12

Virginia studied Jermaine for the
next three hours of the ride in an attempt to
understand what he was going through. The
world seemed to be a simple place in her
own mind, so when someone else seemed to
be confused it left her bewildered. Losing a
wife in that way would have to leave a deep
scar on a person. In the end did it really
matter how they went? Virginia wondered.
Everyone in this little caravan has lost
people. Al and Zoe had just lost a son and
great nephew, yet they were still
functioning. Jermaine seemed to be lost in
his own world. For the last few hours he had
stared blankly out the window at the passing
countryside. The rest of the group observed
and commented as to how the herds seemed
to be growing larger. Jermaine just stared
out his window. Not even Zeus, laying his
head down on Jermaine's knee, got any sort
of reaction. In Virginia's mind it was all so
easy to understand. The weak died, only the
strongest and smartest were still alive. The
pandemic cleaned out or changed the weak
into those creatures who, in turn, ate the
surviving weak. She killed them because
they were weaker and dumber than she was.
There was no doubt in Virginia's mind that

most of the people traveling with her and Lori would not make it. In fact, they were probably on borrowed time because they were with them. Maybe she herself was on borrowed time thanks to Zeus and Perseus. There were numerous times that the lads had saved her, or led her away from things that would have caused her harm. It occurred to Virginia that it was possible she and the lads weren't strong by themselves. Maybe it was the group that made them strong, and failing to be a part of the group was what made people like Taquisha weak and vulnerable. It was safer with Lori and the rest of the group around.

Having been so deep in thought, Virginia failed to notice that Jermaine was smiling at her as he petted Zeus.

"This big guy hasn't so much as given me the time of day other than to growl at me before today. He sure came through when I needed him though, didn't he? So did you, little one, and I will never forget what you have done for me for as long as I live," Jermaine added with tears slowly traveling down his face.

Virginia smiled back at Jermaine, glad to see that he was coming back from wherever it was that his mind had been. "I think the lads have grown used to you being in their way all of the time," Virginia replied as she began to laugh.

"I don't care what their reasons or yours, thank you," Jermaine added.

"I was wondering about something, and I am not sure how to ask it," Virginia said just low enough for Jermaine to hear.

"You can ask me anything you want after today."

Virginia thought for a moment how she could put it into words, and then took a sly look around at the others in the RV to make sure that no one was paying attention to her or Jermaine. Satisfied that the others were more worried about the herd size outside the windows, she continued, "Do you think that people have a destiny?"

Jermaine leaned forward toward Virginia and whispered loud enough for her to hear, "We all make our own destiny. There is nothing for certain in life."

"Then we decide if we live or die?"

"The Lord may have a large hand in that, but for the most part, whether you do or don't do something stupid enough to get yourself killed is up to you and only you."

Jermain reached out and picked up Virginia's hand, holding it gently in his massive hand. "So if your next question is if today was Taquisha's destiny, the answer is no. Taquisha picked this end for herself, and, in a way, I can respect her for that. She wasn't made for the world we live in now. I don't know for sure if any of us are made for it. What I do know is that you have become *too* made for this. You are letting a lot of what makes us who we are go past you, and replacing it with hate. When you kill one of them creatures, do it well. But always remember once they are no more that at one time it was someone's mom or dad, brother, sister or friend that had dreams and aspirations."

"I don't know that world anymore most of the time. I can barely remember what my mother and father looked like, Jermaine."

Jermaine smiled warmly at her and said, "Looking at you and your sister, I think you could be safe to look in the mirror and see the face of your mother, and shades of your father mixed in."

"Sometimes Lori used to talk about them, but I couldn't remember the things she would talk about. I remember the creature that the men dragged out of our house as both of them."

"Didn't you have a brother too? What about him?"

"I mostly remember seeing the blood soaked ground when I first started killing the creatures, and Bob rescuing us."

"This Bob you describe, he sounds like a standup guy," Jermaine replied.

Virginia seemed to lose herself in memories of Bob for a few minutes and was only brought out by the RV slowing.

"Looks like Lori wants to talk," Al called out from the driver's seat.

Virginia could see the headlights of the truck heading back toward them on the other side of the road, going past the RV, and then returning alongside it. Jermaine opened the window nearest the truck and stuck his head out into the cold breeze, squinting at Lori.

"We can see lights on in a building that I think is Rivers Crossing," Lori stated with a smile.

"Lights? You really see lights on?" Al asked from his window.

Lori tried to contain her own joy at the prospect of being at a place that still had electricity and running water. "Not only that, but it looks like there is a set of head lights up ahead of us as well."

"It would be good to get out and stretch our legs in safety. I don't know about the rest of you, but I have been cooped up with you guys for a little longer than I am comfortable with," Pam said from in the RV.

"What about all of this?" Jermaine asked, motioning at the herd that surrounded them.

"Not sure what we will find when we get there. For electricity, I think we could take the building if the creatures have it."

Jermaine nodded in agreement with Lori. He was certain that they could take it if needed.

"Ok, I wanted to let everyone know that we are almost there. Looks like the herd is getting larger, so we will need to keep together and keep moving. I am not sure if we stop, that we could get moving again. There are a lot down there, and I mean a lot," Lori said as she pressed down on the gas pedal, sending the truck lurching forward in the snow.

******

CHAPTER 13

The first official meeting of the new Rivers Crossing Council was held in the cafeteria with all of the survivors present. Doc gave a speech that explained why the first council had been selected, including why each person on the council had been chosen. He made it painstakingly clear to all present that there would be elections to replace half of the appointed council members in six months' time, and then in twelve months, to replace the other half. That way, Doc explained, the business of running the town wouldn't come to a standstill because all six members were running for reelection. Only half would be up per election that would be held every six months afterward. There were no complaints made known during or after the speech as far as Charlie could tell.

Their first meeting held votes on positions that Doc felt were needed to keep the survivors going. They voted on having maintenance, housekeeping, defense, resource acquisition and education; all things that Charlie believed were important. Judging by the reactions from the nearly one hundred survivors, they thought so too. Doc and Boo had hit this nail on the head. The survivors were more alive tonight than Charlie had seen them since before the world went to pieces. The most time was spent on defense, with Boo taking over the podium from Doc. By the time he was finished, there were twenty volunteers for the newly formed Rivers Crossing Guard Corps; twenty-two if you counted Boo and himself in the final tally. Deep down Charlie was okay with helping keep the place safe from the creatures, not putting up too much of an argument when Boo asked him to help out with it by being his second in command.

It would allow Charlie to keep to himself for a while, either on watch in the eagles' nest, or on the proposed rounds through the town. That was okay with him; he was still having a lot of issues in his head that he was trying to sort out since that last day with Annie in the house. There were times when he woke up and started to speak to her, only to realize that she wasn't lying on the right side of the bed. Doc told him that was all part of the grieving process and not to worry too much on it.

When the meeting had finally come to a close, Charlie looked over at Boo and said, "I think I will take the first eight hour watch in the eagles' nest."

"I wasn't starting that until tomorrow, after we meet with all of the new members, Charlie."

"No time like the present; I can use some time alone, Boo," Charlie stated as he rose from the table.

"Charlie, there is an open barrel and some firewood up there in the center of the roof. Light that so you have someplace to get some warmth when you need it," Boo said. "Also, grab that old hunting rifle of yours, and some shells. Might as well do some good if the need arises and you see something that needs to be dropped."

Charlie shook his head in agreement and made his way through the crowd of survivors. People that had known him his whole life, and a few that had not, reached out and shook his hand vigorously. *Doc was right*, he said to himself again. *This is exactly what this place needed to get on its feet again.*

The hallway and the narrow stairs leading up to the roof were a welcome respite from it all. It was empty and Charlie welcomed the loneliness of it. At the top of the stairs he could hear a set of footsteps coming up behind him. One was heavier

171

than the other and moving fast while the quieter set was slow and steady. Ignoring them, he went out into the heavy wind, straight over to the barrel. Boo had left everything he needed to get the fire going, which made Charlie wonder if Boo had planned on being up there tonight. That was fine by him, he liked being around Boo. The door behind him swung back open and the largest man Charlie had ever seen burst forward, running to the edge, barely even noticing the fire or Charlie. Instinctively, Charlie reached for the rifle that he had left just inside the doorway. Noticing that he didn't have it, Charlie moved toward the door quietly when the second person came through. It was Tressa, from the council meeting. Giving a quick embarrassed wave she moved on to the large man at the edge.

"Not so fast, Todd! It is slippery up here," Tressa stated.

"It's not so bad, Tressa. I have on those good running shoes that you gave me, and they don't slide at all!"

"Ok, Todd, just be careful or we will have to go back downstairs where it is a little safer."

"I will behave, Tressa, you don't have to worry. We can see more up here than we can downstairs," the large man replied.

Tressa turned back toward a completely bewildered Charlie and said, "Sorry about barging in on you. Todd can see patterns like no one I have ever met before. His favorite is the stars, so we have been coming up here just to look up at the night sky when it has been clear enough. To be honest, even on the overcast nights we come up here. He can find patterns to amaze himself in just about anything."

"That's fine, I just didn't expect anyone else to come up here," Charlie replied. "I am afraid you're not going to see very many stars tonight with this snow storm coming in."

Tressa shrugged her shoulders, "Then we will just end up looking at the zombies again. Yay us."

"Why does he look at the creatures?" Charlie asked.

Again, Tressa shrugged her shoulders and patted Todd on the back, "Todd, why do we look at the zombies?"

"I don't look at the nasty creatures, Tressa!" Todd replied with a snort as he rolled his eyes and did a little eye shift toward Tressa so that Charlie could see. It was as if he was saying to Charlie, *Can you believe this?* Charlie thought.

"What do you look at then, err... uh, Todd is it?" Charlie asked.

Todd pointed out toward the old Miller farm and said, "They are all in patterns or groups, you see? They always stay together no matter where they are. Some move in, to the bigger group, making a larger pattern, but they always stay together. Except that group, you see them in the middle? They are the biggest group here; they go all over without the others."

"So you think that this mass of creatures is a bunch of smaller masses?" Charlie asked.

Todd whirled around on him excitedly causing Charlie to jump back, almost losing his footing in the snow. "Careful there or Tressa will not let us come up here, Mister," Todd stated as a matter of fact with a frown on his face. "Maybe we need someone to shovel all this snow off so it would be safe? Maybe that someone could be me, Mister?"

"Sure, you can shovel all you want up here, if it is ok with Tressa. First, tell me about the big group," Charlie replied.

"Okay, it's like this Mister," Todd stated as he got down on his hands and knees and started drawing a large shape with smaller ones inside of it surrounding another large shape in the middle. Then he put an "X" in all of the shapes except the one in the middle and said, "All of these move in tight every night with the others. The group is always larger at night than day, you follow me Mister? But this group moves around at night instead of during the day. They come right outside of this building every night and look at the fence down there."

"You're saying that a large group comes here to the school?"

Todd rolled his eyes yet again, only this time at Charlie, "Not all of them Mister. Only a few come here by us, the rest wait just at the end of the streets."

"Have you seen them Todd?" Charlie asked impatiently.

"Yes Sir, I have seen them when Tressa is quiet enough so as not to spook them off. They go all along the fence, playing with it."

Tressa thought that this had been enough excitement for Todd. She would never get him to go to sleep tonight if this kept up. All night long she would have to hear about patterns within patterns. "Todd, we should be going back downstairs if you want to have that pudding before we go to bed tonight," Tressa stated.

"Mister, I have to go so that I can get my night-time snack. Can I come up here with you again sometime, if Tressa says it's okay?"

"Yes Todd, I would like that," Charlie replied smiling at the small child trapped in a large man's body.

Todd lifted himself up and started to dust the snow off and said, "Race you downstairs, Tressa! Last one there doesn't get a snack before bed!" He was off in the same mad dash that had brought him onto the roof.

"Thank you for listening to him, Charlie. It means a lot to him when people talk to him like he knows what he is talking about."

"My pleasure; I think I may have learned something from Todd that we needed to know," Charlie replied.

After watching Tressa and Todd go through the door to the stairs and warming up a few minutes by the fire barrel, Charlie walked over to where Todd had been standing. The snow was starting to come down pretty heavily now so the pattern was all but covered up. Ominously, the center group was still visible, and Charlie wondered what it was that made that group behave differently than the other groups that made up the herd.

Looking back out at the herd at Millers farm, Charlie thought for a minute that he too could see the patterns that Todd spoke of; he closed his eyes in amusement at the thought. All he could see in front of him was a bunch of smelly dead creatures that didn't get the memo telling them that they were dead. Still, Todd did see something, or thought he saw something. Wouldn't hurt to look into it a little more or keep an eye out for any of them coming up to the fence at night. That was unsettling in so many ways that Charlie couldn't even pick which one would be at the top of his list. All it would take would be for one person to not secure the gates leading into the school and that would be it. Caught sleeping, the survivors would be an easy meal for the creatures. They would wake up to either the reek of the zombies upon them or the pain from a chunk of flesh being ripped away. Then Charlie remembered that the school was built up so they would have to climb stairs. Even though he could swear that the one he shot was coming down the stairs just fine, unlike his beloved Annie. Boo had told him that in times like that the mind fills in the gaps that it couldn't account for. He had shot the creature as it was falling down the stairs, but his mind told him that it was walking down them.

The door creaked open behind Charlie and slammed shut, giving him a start. It was Boo, coming up to join him on watch for a few hours. Part of Charlie was glad to have the company, the other part knew that this was Boo's way of making sure the job got done the way he would do it. Either way, Charlie was glad to have him up there.

"It is cold up here, Charlie. Maybe we should have two barrels," Boo stated.

Charlie shrugged his shoulders and replied, "Maybe a warming hut would be better than having two barrels. Put two guys up here so one can watch while the other warms up."

"Next thing you know you will be asking for a coffee pot and a recliner, Charlie."

"I was going to wait until you got settled in as the Commander of the guard before I started asking for the luxury items," Charlie replied laughing.

"That's you, Charlie, always looking out for me."

Something had caught Boo's eye as he scanned the horizon, pulling his attention away from Charlie. "Look, out there along the highway, Charlie. Do you see what I see?"

Focusing on where Boo had pointed, Charlie couldn't see anything at first, but then it was there plain as day. "Headlights! There are headlights just south of the Miller place."

"Look a little further west. There are three more sets, too."

Charlie followed the road to where it just rose up on top of a little hill and there were three more sets of headlights coming down the road. "Should we go down to the bridge and meet them?" Charlie asked.

"Let's wait until they are almost to the bridge; too damn cold to stand out there tonight."

Charlie wanted to go now and make sure that they got into town safely. For all of his talk about leaving in the spring, and being out in the world on his own for the first time in his life, Charlie liked to have people in large numbers around him since the apocalypse had happened. There was something about knowing that others were feeling like he was that made him feel better about the situation. If asked a few days ago, he might have felt differently. Today he had met Tressa and Todd, was part of the assembly in the cafeteria, and now he too felt like he was a part of something. He had to give it to Doc and Boo when it came to that; this place was alive for the first time today, and Charlie was getting caught up in it too.

"Charlie, does it look to you like that first set of headlights are coming to a stop?" Boo asked.

Charlie squinted in an attempt to see better then replied, "It sure does, Boo. And why in the hell would they be stopping there? They have nothing but open space from there all the way to the bridge?"

"Not sure, Charlie. Unless they are having motor troubles or ran out of gas. We will keep an eye on them. If it looks like they are stuck there we will head out and bring 'em in."

Charlie nodded his head in agreement, then remembered that there were binoculars down in their sleeping quarters. "I will be right back, Boo," he stated as he ran off to get them.

****

CHAPTER 14

The going had been at a slow, but steady, pace so far. Lori thought that they were possibly closing the gap between themselves and the headlights ahead. Then it dawned on her that the headlights were stopped in the middle of the road. It even looked like the little car had backed up so that the rear hatchback was facing off to the farm. That was when Lori realized that two people had gotten out of the car and were running toward the herd. Not wanting to believe that she was seeing two more suicides by zombie, Lori strained her eyes to see what they were running to. Nothing jumped out in an obvious way, so she began to worry if the bus and RV would be able to navigate around the car. From where she was now it didn't look like it, but they were still a little ways off. Her first thought had been to slow down and give the car time to do whatever the two outside of it were planning to do. If they were committing suicide she could nudge it from the road and the problem was solved. Then Lori saw what they were doing—rather she heard it first. A shot rang out and a dog sized creature fell to the ground. Lori knew that would bring the herd closer to the farm, and down on them quickly.

The two were trying desperately to drag whatever they had shot back to the car. A third person exited the car and opened the rear hatch, waving them on. As they grew closer, Lori could see that it was a small woman no older than herself. The two dragging what she could now see was a pig, were not making much headway at all. The herd was closing in fast, and Lori knew soon it would be too late for them. Pulling up behind the car she yelled out her window to the woman, "They don't have time to drag that thing back here. Get them out of there before it's too late!"

The woman waved Lori off as if she was meddling in their business and needed to go on her way; Lori would gladly have done so, if it wasn't for the beat up old Chevette blocking the path. Closing the final distance between them, Lori could see that there were children in the back seat staring blankly at her and the truck. Slamming the truck into park, she grabbed her bow and climbed out. Taking aim at the zombies closest to the two figures, Lori began dropping them to the ground. Virginia and a few of the others joined her, dropping as many zombies as they could. Soon the futility of it began to become apparent as the two figures were surrounded and disappeared from their view. The woman at the back of the car pulled out a handgun and began firing wildly at the herd. Lori wasn't sure if she was actually doing any damage to the zombies. It was more likely that she was calling the zombies to them. This was not a place that Lori or the others wanted to be. There were just too many zombies in this herd to fight off with any chance of walking away. Lori grabbed the woman's arm with one hand while taking the gun away from her with the other.

"If you don't want you or your children to die here, you need to get in that car and drive as fast as you can!"

There was no answer from her, just a cold blank stare with tears running down her face. Lori began to tell the others to grab the kids from the car, but it was too late. The herd had converged around all but the back of the Chevette now. Had it not been for Virginia and the others, Lori might have been pulled into the herd as well. The woman broke free of Lori's grasp and ran to help her children, which was the last Lori saw of her as she went down.

"There are too many, Lori! We have to go now!" Virginia yelled.

Lori looked around and could see that even while using nearly everything they had, they were unable to hold the encroaching herd back. "Get in the cars; we'll make a run for it!"

The others fell back to the bus and RV, fighting their way through the beginnings of the herd. While they were taking care of the wave coming from the farm, another group moved in on their flank from the field on the opposite side of the road. For the first time, it seemed like their luck had run out; today would be the day that they all bought the farm.

In the safety of the truck, Lori could see just how desperate the whole situation had become. It looked like the bus was loaded up again, but Virginia and Jermaine were standing outside of the RV still fighting. A broadside, fired out the windows of the RV, sent the herd sprawling backward a little as the zombies in front were knocked to the ground. Lori watched as Virginia scampered back into the RV with Jermaine close behind.

Now that everyone was safely in a vehicle, Lori started the truck back up and tried to move forward. Giving it a little gas, then some more, the truck groaned against the mass of animated dead bodies until it reached the Chevette. For a moment, Lori could see the pieces of flesh that had been tossed about in the initial feeding frenzy. Trying to force that from her mind, she pushed the gas pedal a little harder. The herd had grown so large that it was like shoving a mountain out of the way. The little car moved a little then settled into a stubborn rest. The snowy road offered no traction for the truck's rear wheels, and it started to look like they might have to back their way out of there. Trying to look behind her, Lori couldn't see if the bus was boxed in as well. Even if it wasn't, there would be no way to tell them what she wanted them to do now.

******

CHAPTER 15

By the time Charlie returned with the binoculars he could see without them that the situation had become dire. The tops of the bus, RV, and the pickup truck were still visible, but the small car seemed to have vanished under a sea of zombies. Every now and then a burst of gunshots would ring out. The herd would shift a little then close back in, filling the gap.

"It looks like we don't have to worry about meeting them at the bridge," Boo stated.

"I agree. Maybe we should head out there and offer some help getting through there."

"Charlie, you barely held it together with a few coming at you in the preacher's house! That is a whole different ball game out there right now. They are coming from everywhere!" Boo yelled at him.

"So we just let them die out there?"

"Charlie, I feel for them too. Do you want to add two more bodies to the body count?" Boo asked, trying to defuse the situation a little.

"No, I do not!" Charlie exclaimed. "Boo, you do what you want, but I am going out there and bringing them in!"

Charlie grabbed his old hunting rifle and headed to the door as fast as he could without losing his footing in the fresh snow cover. "Charlie, hold on a second. I think I have a plan that just might work!" Boo yelled at him, causing Charlie to slide in the snow as he stopped and turned around. Charlie stood there staring blankly, waiting for Boo to reveal the plan.

"Meet me down at the dump truck. You know the old village one with the plow on the front?"

Charlie shook his head yes, even though he was somewhat bewildered by Boo's choice to use that old thing.

"On your way down there, grab the AR-15s that I taught you to shoot, and enough ammo to last us. If you ain't struggling from the weight of it, you don't have enough. Now get moving, Charlie, if you want to save those people!"

Feeling like he had just been scolded, Charlie ran down the stairs into their dorm room and grabbed the two AR-15s, stuffing boxes of ammo into the coat pockets of the old winter parka. Charlie was in a mad dash down to the main level, as he passed other survivors who jumped out of his way. Once outside, he ran as fast as he could on the snowy ground, expecting to be at the truck ahead of Boo, and possibly grabbing the driver's seat. Boo tended to do things well, but at his own pace. Charlie didn't feel like this was a time to be cautious, they need to be quick. Unfortunately for Charlie, Boo was climbing into the driver's side as Charlie made it to the truck. Without a word, Charlie opened the door and set the AR-15s into the cab before he climbed in himself. Boo was sitting there smiling as he waited for the light to go off telling them that the glow plug had warmed up enough to start the old diesel engine.

The engine roared to life with a puff of thick black smoke exploding from the exhaust pipe. Grinding the gears as he tried to find first, Boo started the truck up with a small lurch, sending them on their way.

Charlie felt like he was the cavalry in some old black and white western movie. Even fear couldn't dampen the excitement that passed through his body at the prospect of saving the day and bringing those people to safety.

"Charlie, when we get over the bridge we're going to plow our way through everything that gets in our way; we'll have the advantage of having cleaned the road off for the return trip home," Boo said with a big smile.

Charlie nodded his head in agreement with the plan, despite the fact he wasn't quite sure how it was going to work. The one thing he had learned was that Boo Peterson didn't do anything without thinking it out first. Knowing that raised his expectations of the plan's success rate more than just a little bit. Once they reached the opposite side of the main Street Bridge, Boo stopped the truck and lowered the plow to the road.

"This is where we can turn back, Charlie, if you're having second thoughts," Boo stated.

Charlie thought for a few minutes on the gravity of what they were about to do and the utter craziness of it, "I don't think that I could live with myself if we didn't try, Boo."

"That's good to hear, Charlie, because we may not live for trying," Boo replied as he started to pull forward. Out of habit, Boo turned the knob on the radio to the on position and started looking for a station to listen to. Finding only static, he turned to Charlie and stated, "We're going to have to find an old eight track player for this thing."

When Charlie failed to see the humor in it, Boo started to explain about eight tracks, then thought better of it. He had seen plenty of young men go into battle for the first time, and he knew Charlie was sorting it all out in his head right now.

"Charlie, did it look like this group was this large from the roof?" Boo asked.

Charlie shook his head and said, "No, I think it has grown in size since we were looking."

"Makes you wonder exactly how many there are out here in the farms."

"Now that you mention it, I was just thinking that also. How do we hold off anything this big? Do we have enough guns and ammo to keep them out of town?"

"Oh, I think we can come up with a few things until the river freezes over. If it freezes over we may have an issue or two come our way," Boo replied. "Get yourself

ready, the fun's about to start now, Charlie!
Keep a very close eye out for that little car. I
don't want to smack into it at this speed."

Charlie shook his head yes and
leaned forward before, "It was right in front
of that pickup truck, so we have a ways to
go yet."

"Yup, about a mile I would guess.
Shows you just how many creatures are out
here, doesn't it?"

Charlie nodded yes as the plow
struck the outside of the herd, sending
bodies and snow flying everyplace. It was
hard to hold in the enthusiasm for Boo's
choice of the old plow truck now. The
zombies were no match for the large truck
moving at forty or fifty miles an hour; it was
cutting a clear path through them. Every
now and then the plow would skip up, off
the ground, and the sound of cold steel on
pavement would be gone; having trapped a
body beneath it. Once the zombie was worn
away or cut in two, the plow would lower
and the sound would return.

Charlie looked behind them and saw
that the herd was closing in on the road
again. It was unsettling at first because it
was their way home, but it passed quickly.

The truck would cut a path through them; going back that way would come just as easily as heading out was going. Boo started to slow the truck down as the pickup grew closer. Charlie could see that no one was left in the small car that he judged to be an old Chevette. Charlie was amazed that there was still one running after all of these years. He had never thought they were a very durable car.

"Charlie, we can't get past that," Boo stated, pointing at the Chevette. "I think we can push it off the road, but that truck is too close to it. I think I would end up pushing it off the road too. Do you think you could climb up on the hood and yell to them to try and backup?"

Charlie thought Boo had lost it and gone completely crazy at first. Then he could see it was the only way to get any type of word to them. He rolled the old window down as best as he could. It was sticking from a year of being in the up position, but finally gave way and lowered. While climbing out the window, the true size and horror of the creatures around him became strikingly apparent. This was so much different than in the preacher's house. Those moments in that house had been the scariest moments in his whole life up until climbing out of that truck window. Finger tips of flesh or bone were brushing against his legs, trying to grab hold of anything reachable. Luckily, the cab sat high enough so that only the tallest zombie could even come close to reaching him. If they had the ability or sense to jump, Charlie knew he would be torn to pieces.

The hood of the old GMC was cold and slippery. It was difficult to find any footing at all. In a half kneeling-half standing position, Charlie yelled, the loudest he could to be hear over the growling and moaning of the herd, at the driver in the truck. He told them to flash the lights if they could hear him.

The lights flashed on and off twice.

"If you can back up so that we can push that car off the road, flash twice," Charlie yelled and then waited. When he saw no flashes he yelled it once more, loud enough to strain his vocal chords. The lights flashed twice and the sound of the engine from the pickup roared as it forced its way back. A little at first, and then enough to try to move the Chevette.

Boo started forward, causing Charlie to slide back into the windshield with enough force to send cracks running in every direction. Charlie turned to look at Boo who shrugged and mouthed the word, "Sorry."

*****

Lori saw the snow plow coming toward them from the town they were heading to. Lights were beaming from the top of the cab, as well as high beams lighting the way as it grew closer. The herd was being shoved out of the way, bodies flying in every direction. The relief she felt at the prospect of being rescued, after all this time struggling to survive wherever they went, was immense. When the plow grew close enough, it came to a sudden stop. A man climbed out of the cab window onto the hood and started yelling something at her. Lori couldn't quite make it out over the noise from the zombies, but she also realized that her window was all the way up. Rolling it down just enough to welcome sound but still keep the zombies out, the words became clearer. Flashing the headlights in response brought an excited response from the man who continued yelling to her. After a few minutes she understood; he wanted her to back up so that they could push the little car out of the way. Lori put the truck into reverse and eased the accelerator pedal

195

down. The engine groaned, but there was no movement. It was like backing up to a cement wall and trying to nudge it back. Easing off the pedal, Lori closed her eyes and gave it more gas on the second attempt, and was rewarded with a slight motion backwards. Once it began to move, the truck picked up little by little until she felt that there was more than enough room for the plow to move the car.

The plow truck backed up so as to angle the plow toward the car and started forward. The Chevette slid out of the way, down into the ditch, opening up the way into town. Not being able to help it, Lori smiled as the large truck worked its way in small bursts of forward and reverse until it was turned around, pointing back to town.

Boo blew the horn to let her know that they were ready to proceed back down the road. Lori answered them with two blows on her horn, and was pleased to hear the same response come from the RV and bus. She let out a sigh of relief hearing both of her vehicles respond.

The plow started back to town when Lori noticed that it was spreading salt too. *Funny that someone would even think about that now in these times*, she thought to herself. Perhaps they didn't want the zombies to slide on the ice. No matter what the reason was Lori wasn't stopping until she was safely out of the herd and into that town.

"Looks like we will have a warm bed for the night," Lori said to the boy she had picked up at the drive-in.

"Looks like it," he replied.

Lori thought for a few minutes and then said, "You know, I don't think I know your name."

"You haven't asked," he replied.

"Ok, well I am asking you now."

"My name is Walter, not Wally, but Walter."

Smiling to herself Lori replied, "Glad to meet you, Walter, not Wally."

The boy laugh at how funny it sounded, "Just 'Walter' will do. Do you think I will get a bed to myself?"

"Don't know yet what kind of accommodations they will have, Walter, but we will sure try to get you one."

*****

The RV rocked like a boat on rough seas as the herd closed in on all sides. It was as if they thought pushing hard enough would force the box open, allowing the meaty morsels inside to be had. Every few minutes, Jermaine would direct everyone with a firearm to fire out one side or the other, causing the herd to falter in its relentless push. It was after one of these volleys that Al yelled out excitedly that they would be "Moving soon!"

Virginia made her way back to the front, having to push past the rest of the group. There she saw the plow shoving the little car out of the way with a crazy man standing precariously on the truck's hood.

"Do you think they came to help us?" she asked Al.

"It sure looks like it! Doesn't matter why they are here, we will take the help anyway," Al said grinning from ear to ear.

"Look, they are plowing the road clear of the herd!" Virginia said to Jermaine.

The RV started to move, following Lori and the plow. It wasn't as easy going as Lori was having; as the plow knocked the zombies out of the way for her, the herd closed back in around the back after she had passed. That didn't stop Al; he pushed the pedal and kept driving straight ahead no matter what got in the way. The RV was no longer rocking from side to side, but more in an up and down motion as it went over the carcasses on the road left in Lori's wake.

CHAPTER 16

The rescue had so far been a success and Boo knew it, even if he wasn't saying much about it. Charlie thought that was odd, considering it had been Boo's plan, but that was Boo.

"Looks like we are going to make it after all," Charlie stated.

"Sure does, Charlie."

"You sound as if you would rather we didn't make it," Charlie added.

Boo shot him a dirty look and then said, "Charlie, how many people do you think are in those three vehicles back there? Do we know what kind of people they are, or what their intentions are?"

"I don't have any more of a way of knowing how many are back there than you do, Boo!"

"That's right Charlie, you don't know! For now, we have to be cautious once we cross the bridge. The last thing we want to do is invite trouble in the front door."

Charlie thought in a small way he could see what Boo was talking about—in a small way. On the other hand, those people were survivors of this messed up world just like they were. If there was a small way that they could help them, then that is what they should do.

The rest of the ride back to the bridge was quiet, with neither of them saying anything. Once they crossed the bridge into Rivers Crossing Boo pulled off into an old, rarely used lot where a used car lot had been for a short time back in the late 80's. He watched as the other three vehicles pulled in behind him. Climbing down out of the truck with his rifle in hand, he made his way slowly to the black truck where the young woman rolled her window down.

"Thank you very much!" she stated. "I thought we were going to have to fight our way out of that mess back there!"

"You're welcome, young lady," Boo replied as he looked her and the kid over. "How many people do you have, and how are you set for supplies?"

Lori thought for a few minutes trying to gauge if this was a safe place to talk about what they had for supplies when she heard a voice from the other side of the truck say, "We have more than enough to pay for our stay." Her head snapped around to see Zoe standing there with Virginia and the lads.

Boo started over to the woman, but backed off seeing Zeus and Perseus. "Nice dogs you have there."

Zoe ignored the comment and replied, "My name is Zoe. This is Virginia, the lady in the truck is Lori, and these two here are Zeus and Perseus."

"Glad to meet you, Zoe. My name is Beau, but everyone around here just calls me 'Boo.' That there in the truck is Charlie. Welcome to Rivers Crossing."

Lori stepping out from the truck asked, "We have over sixty people with us; can you fit us in for a few days?"

"I think we can. We turned an old school and library into a sort of keep, you could say. Plenty of room for everyone there. You will have to talk to the town council about staying, but I am sure they will go along with it." Boo knew that as much as he disagreed, Doc wasn't turning anyone away from Rivers Crossing.

Charlie had finally joined them in front of the trucks, looking agitated that Boo hadn't called him to come out.

"Hi, I am Charlie. Welcome to Rivers Crossing," he stated as he trudged through the snow to meet them. He knew instantly from the dirty look he got from Boo that it was a mistake to leave his gun in the truck.

Charlie knew that Boo worried about things that they all probably should have worried about too. In this case, it was pretty simple to Charlie. They thought they were probably the only ones that survived, and here was proof that there were others. It would seem that the more there were of them, the better chance they had to survive a little longer.

"Well, Charlie, maybe we should lead these folks over to the school so they can meet Doc and the council. Get them fed and bedded down for the night. We can take this conversation back up in the morning," Boo stated.

"I think you're right, Boo. Let's get them moving. Ladies, if you would be so kind as to follow us over to the school," Charlie explained motioning up Main Street.

"Zoe, why don't you go ahead with the others and follow them over. If you would take little Walter with you, and mind you it is Walter, not Wally; Virginia and I will hang back by the bridge a little while and make sure that nothing is following us in."

Zoe nodded her head in agreement and smiled, motioning for Walter to come from the truck with her to the RV.

"Charlie, why don't you go with the ladies here," Boo said.

Before either of them could object, Charlie said yes and walked over by Lori. They watched as the vehicles pulled out and headed off to the school. A lone figure stood over where the RV had been parked and started coming toward them. Charlie reached for his gun and remembered he had left it in the plow cab.

"I thought you would stay with us," Lori stated to the large figure coming toward them.

"I wanted to stretch my legs a little before we got wherever we are going,"

"If you were worried about the ladies being safe out here with me, you didn't have anything to worry about," Charlie said.

The man broke out in a wild sounding laugh and he was laughing so hard that tears were running down his cheeks.

"Friend, if these two dogs didn't want you near them, or thought you would harm to this little girl, you would be on the ground in a whole lot of pain. If—now if—they let you pass to get to her, and she didn't want you there... you would wish that the dogs had taken care of you before she got to you. And that little lady there, well, I am not sure you would ever consciously know that you hit the ground, or even if your last thoughts on earth would be how you got to that point. You could say I am here to keep you safe," Jermaine stated, laughing the whole time. Then as suddenly as he had started laughing he stopped and turned to Lori and Virginia. "You think they will follow us in?"

"That has been the story in the past. They follow the food once they have caught the scent."

"That's what I was afraid of, too," Jermaine replied.

"If you want to keep an eye on them, we have the perfect spot. We don't have to stand on the bridge to do it. On the roof of the school we can see in all four directions. That's how we saw you guys coming down the road behind that little car."

"If we could see everything, Lori, it would be better," Virginia added.

"Okay, we will go over to your school and see what we can see from up there," Lori decided. "How far up the road is it?"

"It's about two blocks. Once you pass that little bend in the road there, you can see the school and library," Charlie replied.

"The lads and I will walk and meet you there," Virginia stated as her and the dogs started down the street.

"Are you sure that's a good idea?" Charlie asked Lori and Jermaine.

"If there are any zombies between here and the school the dogs will know it, and Virginia will take care of them. If there are any two–point–zeros here, Virginia will let us know when she gets there."

"Two-point-zeros?"

Jermaine couldn't help laughing at Charlie again, "You guys haven't tried to understand or deal with the zombies much here, have you?"

"Just a few here and there, I guess. My wife was one of them," Charlie replied, looking down at the snow remembering his Annie.

"We will teach you everything we know before we move on." Lori said. Then she turned to Virginia and said, "On second thought, I think I would feel more at ease with you and the dogs with me."

Virginia rolled her eyes and started to object, but deep down she agreed with Lori that maybe it would be best to stay together.

Lori handed the keys to the truck to Charlie. "You know the way."

CHAPTER 17

The drive to the school was a little too quiet for Virginia. The town's streets were snow covered like earlier parts their journey had taken them through. Only she really had not paid a lot of attention to the buildings passing by the window. Here it reminded her of a ghost town blanketed in white. There were no signs of life other than the lights coming from the building that the new guy called the school. It made her feel uneasy for some reason that she couldn't quite put her finger on. It may have eased her mind had she walked down the street with the lads to get a closer look, but hopefully there would be time for them to do a little exploring later.

They slowly rolled up on a corner where two of the buildings were set considerably higher than everything else. One was lit up on all three floors, beckoning them to come inside. Charlie turned on the street between the buildings, and then into an opening in the fence to what was clearly a full parking lot. Virginia could see both the RV and the bus up close to the door.

"Well, we are here. Welcome to what we have been calling home," Charlie stated as he turned the key to off and exited the truck. Virginia and the lads jumped down out of the bed and waited for Lori to join them.

"Are we sure we want to go in there?" Virginia asked. "We really don't know what is waiting in there."

"We know what is out there, and it sure couldn't be worse than that," Lori replied.

Charlie motioned for them to follow him and headed to the door. On the way, Lori noticed that no one closed the gate coming into the lot behind them, and there wasn't a soul watching the door in front of them. When they reached it, there wasn't even a lock set on it; Charlie just pulled it open. They could all feel the heat smack them in the face. It had to be at least eighty degrees Fahrenheit, and it took their breath away for a few seconds.

"Okay, this is the main floor here," Charlie said after they climbed the ten well-worn wooden steps just beyond the door. "Down at the end of the hallway, you will find another set of stairs that go down to the front entrance of the building. Next to that is the old school nurse's office that is now Doc's medical room, and another set of stairs that go down into the gymnasium/cafeteria. The kitchen and the showers are also down there. You can get a hot shower every other day in the morning."

"The other rooms here are the family dorms; we try to keep families together. The second floor is mixed between families and singles, with one classroom being used for classes. The third floor is where Doc has been putting the singles, like him and myself."

"A hot shower would be great!" Jermaine stated.

"You may want to get up early then. The line forms quick," Charlie replied laughing. "You can go ahead and look around if you like. Doc usually welcomes everyone new and helps find you a room."

From off to the left of Charlie, a thunderous noise came from the stairs going up to the second and third floor. Before they could identify if it was a threat, the largest man Virginia had ever seen was on top of them.

"Mister, Mister, Doc says you should bring these folks up to the third floor so they can settle in first. OHHHHHH you have puppies!" The man shouted with glee as he fell to his knees and threw his arms around Zeus. Zeus licked his face, wagging his tail; that told Virginia that this was no threat in the lad's mind. That made him safe to her as well.

"This excited fella here is Todd. He is harmless, in case you haven't figured that out yet," Charlie stated smiling.

"Looks like you have a room upstairs with the rest of us singles then," said Charlie.

"No! That lady, Miss Zoe, said you were all part of her family and needed to stay together. Doc said that only real families like me and Tressa could stay in the family rooms, but Miss Zoe wouldn't hear it. She was like Tressa, where I think I can do something and she says 'no way.' Mister could see that he lost and put them all in your room. I asked Tressa if we could stay in that room too, and Mister said, 'why not!'"

"All right then, Todd, why don't you show these folks to their room then," Charlie said, laughing a little at Todd's excitement.

"I sure will, Mister," Todd replied, then started to frown a little. "Can the puppies stay up there, too?"

"Yes Todd, go ahead and take them up as well. Looks like you guys have your own personal escort now, so I have a few things I want to check out up on the roof, and I will catch up to you all later."

Charlie followed them up to the third floor then crossed the hall to the stairs that led to the roof. Once there, he found Boo looking through binoculars out across the river.

"Well, that didn't go so bad after all," Boo said without even looking at him.

Charlie settled in beside Boo and joined him in gazing off into the darkness. Neither man said anything for a few minutes. They were both going over what had transpired over the last hour or so in their own ways. For Charlie, it had been a great success in rescuing fellow humans in their time of need. To Boo, it was a successful mission that succeeded by luck alone. That was alright with Boo; sometimes luck was all you needed, but next time they might not be so lucky. He couldn't shake something the younger one had said. It had him worried. He was not really sure if this would be the time to bring it up; he was hesitant to take the excitement out of Charlie's good deed.

Boo didn't have to figure out how to bring it up, Charlie did it for him. "The girl said they would follow the food source."

"I heard her, too."

"We're safe in the school?" Charlie asked, still looking into the darkness.

"Yes, I believe we are, in the school and the library," Boo replied. "We will have to check out the old tunnel that goes under the street to make sure it is passable. If so, we could close the gates up so that they are as secure as they can be."

"Wouldn't we be kind of trapped in here then?" Charlie asked.

"Yup."

"You think we could hold out in here?" Charlie dug further for the answers to his questions.

"Nope."

"I thought you said we would be safe in the library and the school."

"Charlie, I did say we would be safe in these two buildings, and we will," Boo replied. "How long we can hold out is a different matter altogether. That depends on food to eat, coal to keep us warm, and gas for the generator, now doesn't it?"

Charlie thought for a few minutes and then replied, "All I have accomplished tonight was to bring hell down on us then, haven't I?"

"I think you hastened it a little. I do believe that it was coming this way all along. How long do you think the creatures could feed off of the livestock out on the farms?"

"I guess I never really thought about that," Charlie replied.

Hearing the change in Charlie's voice as he shifted from a man excited with doing the right thing to the man who had to put the creature down that had once been his wife, Boo felt the need to reassure him. "I think we have a few options left, Charlie. If we use some of the town's abandoned cars we could block the bridges. That takes care of them coming in that way unless the rivers freeze over."

"We could use some of the schools buses to block the viaducts on the other side of town," Charlie added.

Boo smiled at him, "Now you're thinking, Charlie!" It was good to see Charlie in action when he actually thought out an issue. If Boo had his choice, Charlie would be doing more leading around here than following. If only they could convince him to lead, and let Doc deal with the mental and physical health.

"Maybe it is time for your guard unit to start earning their keep," Charlie thought out loud.

"Yes, I agree. We will have to get them together and start posting a few up here and at the gates around the clock."

"Do you think they are ready?" Charlie asked.

"No, not yet, Charlie. But the folks that came in today are just what we needed, I think. As long as someone can convince them to lend us a hand and stay for a while."

"You don't think that they are staying or would help out?"

"Not sure, yet. They operate like a small unit, and look like they have seen a lot more of these creatures up close than we have. We should bring it up to them tomorrow morning and get a better idea of what their plans are."

"Plans? What plans could they possibly have that would take them away from here and out there in the middle of that?" Charlie pointing toward the herd.

"From what I hear, they have a map they were following; that is how they ended up here. I guess we will just have to ask them what their plans are, Charlie. From what I have seen so far, if the creatures come into town it would be nice to have them with us."

Charlie agreed on that last point, from what they had both seen out on the road. Those people had stood their ground when the creatures had them completely surrounded. Charlie couldn't tell you with any degree of certainty that he could do the same.

Boo shook his head and handed Charlie the binoculars. "I am going to secure the gates before it gets any later, Charlie. You think you could do a four-hour watch?"

"I can handle it, Boo."

"I will be back up in about four hours then, Charlie. Keep an eye on our gates and the bridges," Boo said as he left.

CHAPTER 18

When they went to bed, thanks to
Lori, Walter was sharing the double bed
with them. He didn't take up much room
and was scrunched up against the window
with Lori in between him and the others.
After getting a good warm meal into their
stomachs, it felt good to sleep in an actual
bed again. Virginia wasn't complaining
about the bunks back at the bunker, or even
about the beds in the RV, but these were real
beds that she could pull the thick blankets up
around her neck and fall into a deep sleep.
Well, she tried to fall into a deep sleep, but it
just wasn't coming as easy as it had for the
rest of the group. It wasn't Zeus' or Zoe's
snoring that was keeping her up, nor the
man called Doc on the other side of the
room harmonizing his snores with them.
Lori was moving around fitfully in her sleep
like she had back at the bunker when Zoe
had saved her. Though even that wasn't
what was keeping her awake. She didn't feel
like they were in any danger, Zeus and
Perseus wouldn't let anything get too near
them. She knew that. There was just
something that felt too good to her, being
around all of these people. In Virginia's
mind there were zombies, people, and

people who didn't know they were soon to be zombies. Being here made her think that maybe there was a chance to live a normal life; a chance to not be as quiet as she could for fear of attracting the zombies to her.

A few hours later Lori began to tremble enough that Virginia felt like she was doing it on purpose, so she sat up and looked over at her sister. Lori's skin seemed to be paler than normal in the little bit of light coming in through the transit above the door from the hallway. Zeus too, had noticed it, and was sitting up staring at her now. Virginia placed her hand softly on Lori's shoulder and shook her. No response. Virginia shook her a little harder until Lori's eyes popped open, causing her to move away quickly. Lori's beautiful eyes had been replaced by black oversized pupils; lifeless eyes like those of a shark. Frozen in time, Virginia didn't know what to do, so she just sat there petrified. Zeus let out a barely audible growl, as if he too was stuck between attacking a zombie or leaving Lori to sleep.

The cold black eyes were locked on Virginia, and she felt what was left of her old life would die soon, and by her own hand. Then she noticed a tear trickle down Lori's cheek.

Walter whispered, "She can't help it. There are too many people here for her to handle."

"What do you mean too many people for her to handle? She's changed!" It was a whisper but is was a whisper full of urgency and panic.

"If we can get her outside to the camper, she will be ok," Walter added as he rolled over and took Lori's hand into his.

Without thinking, Virginia quietly reached down into her backpack, the backpack that held all of the clothes she owned in the world, searching for a dark green hoody. Finding it she tugged it free. "Here, do you think you can help me get this on her?"

Walter took the hoody and began to put it on Lori. Lori took over and completed pulling it over her head. For an instant, Virginia saw her sister and not the creature.

"If we don't run into anyone, I think she will be okay," Walter said as he climbed out of bed. "You know, it is hard controlling it sometimes." Walter pulled Lori's arm until she followed him; they were sneaking out of the room into the hallway. Luckily, there wasn't anyone moving around on the third or second floors. There was some movement at the bottom of the stairs, causing Virginia's anxiety level to rise, but it moved off quickly. The door leading out still wasn't locked in any way; Virginia rolled her eyes in shock. Once they were in the RV, Virginia got the heater started and sat down at the table across from Lori. Walter had laid down on the sofa, looking back at the two of them.

Lori's color was coming back to her now, along with her eye color.

"Is someone going to tell me what the heck happened in there?"

Lori shook her head for a few seconds trying to find a way to tell her baby sister when Walter broke in. "Your sister and I have it in us somehow. Lori was bitten, I think, but I don't remember if I was or not. I don't have any marks, not like she does."

"I think part of that creature is still in me," Lori stated with tears beginning again.

It was a lot for anyone to handle, especially for Virginia who had made it her life's goal to kill all zombies before she died.

"I have watched you since you were on that bus all laid out! I have not seen any sign of a change happening!"

"I know, Virginia. I have been watching myself as well. This is the first time anything like this has happened to me. I have dreams of what I think are things that the creature had seen… but that is it," Lori replied.

"It is the smell, mostly," Walter added. "To us, people or living things smell sweet, like candy. It is hard to explain or control."

"You're right!" Lori stated. "I noticed it when we first got here, but it got stronger when I tried to go to sleep."

"So we have to leave or tell them that the thing that they are trying hard to keep out is sleeping with them in the next bed?"

"I don't know, Virginia!"

"Fine. What else have you noticed since that day? Anything?"

"Sometimes I know they are there before Zeus and Perseus do. Not by a lot, usually under a minute or so," Lori added.

Part of Virginia wanted so badly to put an arrow into Walter and Lori's heads right now before anyone got hurt, or worse. Another part wanted to know if there was a way that Lori could keep going like this and still be Lori.

"You can control this thing?" Virginia asked.

"It is only a tiny part, so I think she can. Just needs to learn how, like I did," Walter replied smiling. "We are still human like you."

"You two should start sleeping in the RV if being around too many people is what caused this. I promise you both, that if you do a full change, I will kill you."

"That is what I would want you to do, Virginia," Lori said with a warm smile.

"I guess if the lads think you're safe to be around, then I do too," Virginia said shaking her head slowly. "The lads and I are going to go for a walk and check things out," she added as she rose up and left without giving Lori a chance to object.

The cold air and solitude outside felt good after hearing all of that in the RV. Not being sure where the walk was going to take them, Virginia decided that she would like to see how good of a view there was on the roof. Pulling the door open and letting the lads enter first, Virginia followed and smacked face first into Boo's chest.

"Bet it is cold out there," he said to her.

"It felt refreshing. I wanted to look around a little."

"If you want to get a good look, why don't you come up and check out the roof? Maybe you can keep Charlie from talking my ear off again," Boo said with a smile.

Virginia nodded her head and followed Boo up to the roof. They were right when they said everything was in view from up there. Once her eyes adjusted to the darkness, she could see the little car where they had been trapped until Boo and Charlie came with the snow plow. More importantly, Virginia could see that the herd had moved surprisingly close to the bridge that they had crossed coming in. Pointing toward them with her finger, Virginia said "Look."

Boo followed the direction that she was pointing when Charlie said, "They're closer to the Jones Street Bridge than the

Main Street Bridge. I am not sure which one we should be more worried about."

"Looks like we need to block the bridges off after all then," Boo stated.

Charlie shook his head in agreement then asked Boo, "Should we be planning for a 'cry uncle' scenario?"

Boo looked at Charlie cold and hard for a few minutes and then said, "What do you think we should do, little lady?"

Virginia didn't even pause to think about an answer, "Stop them before they cross."

Charlie laughed long and hard at that. "How exactly are we going to do that?"

"Use the buses to block the bridges and worry about what gets around them," Boo replied.

"When the rivers freeze over?"

"*If* the rivers freeze over, Charlie; they don't freeze every year," Boo stated as a matter of fact.

Virginia started to walk away from the two men, only stopping at the door when Boo had asked her why she was leaving.

"Looks like we need a few people to help block off your bridges, and I know a few that could help," she said smiling.

Boo and Charlie smiled at her and then each other. "There you go, Charlie, another plan like yours has presented itself," Boo said.

Charlie smiled and replied, "I will get Zach to take the watch from up here and keep an eye on us."

"Good idea, let's all meet down in the lot out back," Boo stated looking first at Virginia who nodded yes, and then at Charlie.

Virginia headed to the third floor and tried to enter their room as quietly as possible. The plan had been to very quietly awaken Jermaine and Albert, leaving Zoe to sleep soundly. That was the plan. Unfortunately, Zoe had heard them leave earlier and was laying awake in her bed.

"What is all this sneaking around in the middle of the night about child?" Zoe asked in hushed tones.

Virginia felt like she had been caught by her mother with her hand in the cookie jar. "Looks like we are going to need to block the bridges off leading into town," Virginia replied.

"I think we all knew that was coming. I was concerned that they didn't know here," Zoe replied as she got out of bed. "Albert, you need to wake up and go help these folks out. Jermaine, rise and shine boy, there is work to be done."

"Is she always this pleasant in the morning?" Jermaine said through a sleepy voice.

"This is a good one. You have no idea what the bad ones are like," Albert replied laughing.

"Virginia, where is your sister at?" Zoe asked. Virginia hung her head a little and looked away from Zoe, "She thought it was too hot in here, so she took Walter and went to sleep in the RV."

Zoe shook her head and said, "I was wondering if this place would cause a problem. You know what I am talking about?" Zoe asked.

Before Virginia could answer, Albert butted in, "There is not very much that gets passed ole Aunt Zoe. You may want to remember that for in the future."

"Ok, where are we going, and what are we about to do when we get there?" Jermaine asked.

"The herd is moving toward the bridges, so we are going to go block them off," Virginia replied as she led them out the door and down the stairs. Once they were outside she was surprised to see Lori and Walter standing by the door waiting for them. Seeing Virginia's look Lori said, "That guy Boo banged on the door and asked us to wait for you, and then to meet them across the street by the library."

Lori took the lead as they crossed over to where three trucks were waiting. One had Boo standing by it talking to three men that Lori had not met yet, while Charlie sat in the cab of the second truck loading a pistol. He smiled at Lori when he had noticed her, causing her to blush a little.

"Welcome to our little party," Boo stated with a large toothy smile.

"Can't say I am overly glad to be here, to be completely honest with you. Of course if it means we don't deal with the creatures on our doorstep, that is a different story," replied Albert laughing.

"I think it will stop them, or buy us a little time to find a better way," Boo said.

"What is the plan then?" Lori asked.

"These guys are going with me over to the Main Street Bridge. We will use what is left of the chain link fencing to create a barrier on the far side of the bridge. If you guys could go with Charlie to see what needs to be done down the street on the Jones Street Bridge, that would be great."

"Virginia or I will go with you. We know what to keep an eye out for," Lori added.

She thought for a minute the old man was going to argue with her until he replied, "Point taken and I agree with you. Is there anything we should know in case we get up close and personal with them?"

Lori looked him in the eyes and said, "If it is only one or two that you are dealing with DO NOT shoot them! All that does is call the others right to you."

"Then what are we supposed to do?" one of the men asked.

"Cave their head in with anything handy. It is the only way to put them down so they stay down," Jermaine replied to the group of men so that they all could clearly hear him. "Is this the first time you have dealt with this?"

"Charlie and I have dealt with them on a limited basis. Most of the others have done their best to stay out of the way," Boo replied.

"Maybe we should get moving so that we can cut down on the chances of changing that. I will go with you guys and cover you while you work. Charlie will be in good hands between Virginia and the dogs, while Jermaine and Albert help him," Lori said as she walked over and climbed into Boo's truck.

"You heard the lady, let's get going fellas," Boo ordered the group.

CHAPTER 19

The sun was just starting to rise off to the east as Boo pulled onto the bridge. In front of him stood a sight that would send fear deep into the soul of most battle hardened veterans, and Boo was no different. It was the type of sight that the mind could not comprehend, that it had no way of processing. With the sunlight to their back the masses of the moving herd looked as though they were glowing. It nearly hid the fact that they were around fifty feet from being on the bridge.

Boo made a U-turn at the far end of the bridge and jumped out of the cab. Opening the tail gate as quietly as he could, he motioned for the others to get out.

"Hank, you grab a few of those ten foot chains there and take them over by the railing on the walk way. Tom, you and Jim give me a hand with the chain link," Boo ordered. When he noticed Hank standing petrified looking at the creatures Boo yelled, "Hank, if you don't get a move on, we will be getting a much closer view of them!"

Hank grabbed the chain and went where he was told to go.

231

The chain link scraped across the bed of the old Ford, causing the herd to go silent. Lori motioned to Boo that they needed to be as quiet as possible. Boo nodded his head yes and then shrugged his shoulders. They dragged the heavy chain link fence roll over to the walkway, loosening the end so that Hank could work the chain through it as best he could, fastening it to the post.

Boo pulled out a padlock and handed it to Hank. "Lock the ends together, Hank, and then get another section of chain."

They rolled it to the first support beam on the bridge, where Hank once again wove the chain through the links in the fence. Lori noticed a lone zombie closing in on them, so she drew an arrow from her quiver and sighted it on the creature. As it grew dangerously close to Boo, she let fly watching the arrow as it found its mark in the side of the skull. The creature fell at the feet of Boo, just between him and Tom.

"You let that one get a little close, didn't you?" Boo joked.

Lori smiled back at him and shrugged her shoulders as he had done earlier, walking over and retrieving her arrow from the skull. Seeing that the herd was within fifteen feet of them now, Lori shouted to Boo, "We need to move quicker! They are too close now!"

"One more beam to latch to, and we are done," Boo replied as the three men unwound the chain link fence across the road. Lori brought down three more zombies as the guys reached the end with just enough fence left. There was a three or four-inch gap, but Boo didn't think anything could squeeze between that, and if it could, there was the length of tow chain fastening it to the beam. They all stood back and looked at their handy work when Boo noticed that the angle of the beams caused the fence to bow downward in the center. Looking around he saw old lady Morris's antique, beat up Volkswagen Beetle parked in front of her house. "Tom, stay here with Lori and help her keep them off the fence. You two meet me over by the beetle," Boo said as he climbed into his truck, starting the engine.

Lori watched as Boo pulled the truck out from behind the beetle. He got out with what looked like a tire iron and smashed the driver's side window in, and reached in, unlocking the door. The three men then pushed the beetle onto the bridge up to the fence, where Boo started to angle it up next to the fence. There, they worked it back and

233

forth until the passenger side was snug up against the fence causing it to bow outward, instead of inward. In all of the excitement Lori had lost track of where the herd was at. When she finally did look out the fence, she could see that they were unbelievably close now.

"How is that for just-in-time suspense?" Boo asked.

"Do you think it will hold?" Hank asked as he backed toward the middle of the bridge, making it clear that he was ready to get off.

"I think it will hold for now," Boo replied looking over at Lori. "We will post someone down here to signal us if it doesn't."

"That would be the best idea, just in case they do push it down," Lori added.

Before Boo could say another word, Tom spoke up, "I will take the first watch if I can come back with something to sit in, and something that I can use to warm up a little every fifteen or twenty minutes."

Boo thought about it for a few minutes, looking up at the sky in that way people do. He looked like he thought the answer was waiting for him to pluck it right from the clouds.

"I will send Hank back with Smithy's tow truck. Hank can follow him in my truck to give him a ride back."

"That will do just fine, Boo. I always wanted to drive that thing," Tom replied grinning.

"All kidding aside, Tom, if they start to push through that fence and that bug starts sliding, push them back with the tow truck." Tom shook his head yes, confirming that he understood what to do.

*****

Charlie *did* have a plan for his bridge. He was still not used to the idea that they were not using the school buses to block them off. Boo had told him that the 'cry uncle' scenario would require the buses to get all of the people out of Rivers Crossing if it came to that. When Boo put it that way, there wasn't a whole lot of argument that Charlie could come up with. In the meantime, he was being drawn to the idea of using the empty fifty-five gallon drums that they were saving to collect gas for the generator. Knowing how Boo would react to that was one of the reasons that

Charlie had kept the idea to himself, until now. Charlie thought Boo had given himself the easy bridge to work with. Strong iron beams running all over the place while Charlie had the early 80's concrete bridge with only concrete sides. No place to fasten a fence or anything else to it, hence the metal drum idea. They could line them up across the road, and then use the fresh water pump to fill them with water. Allowing for expansion, the water would freeze and they would be too heavy to just push out of the way. The bridge was just barely wide enough to fit two modern day, mid-sized cars on it going in opposite directions. Even then, the two cars were awfully close when they passed, causing the drivers to have to slow down to a crawl.

After pulling into the lot behind the library and hooking up the homemade trailer that held the empty barrels in it to the truck, Charlie headed down to the bridge. Once they went through the train viaduct they could get a clear view of the bridge, which was just roughly a football field's distance from the viaduct.

Moving around on the bridge, there were close to fifty zombies. They were just aimlessly wandering around, but they were still there in Charlie's way. Stopping the truck, Charlie let out a loud sigh and felt like all was lost at that point. Just on the other side was what looked like hundreds of zombies just standing there, waiting for anything to come by.

"Well, that is a real problem," Albert said.

"Maybe we can block the bridge on this side?" Charlie asked the group, still shocked.

"We can move them off the bridge. How long to fill the drums?" Virginia asked.

Charlie shook his head no as he replied, "Not quick enough to get it done before the rest of them come on to the bridge."

"Those gas cans full in the bed?" Jermaine asked pointing behind him.

"I don't think that is going to help us, Jermaine," Albert said pointing down at the water where Zombies were already walking across.

"I didn't think that they could cross water!"

"They can't swim, but they can walk just fine! How deep is that?" Virginia asked.

Charlie rose up in his seat so that he could get a better view, "This time of year, depending on the weather, it can be a few inches there or several feet."

"Looks like it is just a few inches to me, and they are moving across it just fine!" Jermaine stated.

Charlie's mind was racing now. The whole reason for saving the bridge was to have access to the water, without which there wasn't a really good way to bring water into the school.

"Any ideas?"

"We can go back and block off the viaduct. That should stop them for now," Albert replied, looking for input from the others.

Charlie shook his head yes as he put the truck into reverse and began to back up toward the viaduct. He knew that Boo wouldn't be happy with this one bit, but there really wasn't another option left. It would open up a Pandora's Box of issues that would have to be addressed but at that moment those were not Charlie's concern.

Once on this side of the river all that stood between the creatures and them was the embankment the train tracks were on, and the levy. The latter wasn't even complete anymore as people took down sections here and there to get a river view from their homes.

Just as they backed through the viaduct, Boo's truck pulled up with him slamming it into park, bringing it to a sliding stop.

"Charlie, what the hell is going on here?" Boo shouted over to Charlie.

Charlie shook his head and yelled back, "The river is too low! Damn thing is only a few inches deep off to the right of the bridge."

Boo shook his head angrily, "I told the mayor that we needed to have that dredged out again. Damn fool said no boats go pass that bridge, so there was no need for it!"

"Boats? No. Creatures coming across? Yes," Charlie stated.

"What do you guys propose we do then?" Boo asked.

"We were thinking about blocking off the viaduct and keeping them on the other side."

Boo turned to Hank and said, "Take Charlie's truck and drop the tow truck off with Tom. Then go over to the creek bridge and use those barrels to block either side of it. You guys pick which side looks like it would work best. Take that hand pump and fill them with water, okay?" Both men nodded their head that they understood and left.

Boo joined the rest of the group looking through the viaduct at the herd moving across the bridge and river.

"Why don't we use that old van there to block it off on the outside over there?" Charlie pointed over to the far side where he was sure that no matter how hard they pushed against the van it wouldn't move an inch if it was set up against the sides.

"Not a bad idea, really. We could easily pull it away if we needed to get through there," Jermaine added.

Charlie shook his head in agreement and then sprinted over to the van. Once inside, he was glad to see that Boo had insisted that any vehicle in the school lot have a key in it, just in case they needed to use it. Anyone still alive that didn't want to leave a key in their car was welcome to park it up the street away from the school. This old clunker didn't belong to anyone that was alive as far as Charlie knew, nor did he care at the moment. He turned the key, and with a sputter, the old V8 roared to life and he threw it into gear. Within a few minutes the short nose of the van was against one wall, and the tail end was against the other side. Charlie went through making sure that all of the doors were locked on the passenger side. Not that he thought the creatures were smart enough to open them; he just didn't want to take that chance.

Walking back to the group, Charlie could see the faces plastered against the windows of the school and the small crowd that had formed against the fence. Pointing to them he told Boo, "This is going to be a problem, Boo."

CHAPTER 20

Virginia was amazed at just how prophetic Charlie had been earlier. The one they called Doc had insisted on having a meeting with everyone, except the people that Boo had put on guard duty around the school and bridges, attending. They were packed into the gymnasium like sardines, with more people sitting on the stairway leading down to the area. Doc had given a long speech about how they had all but beat the odds so far to make it there, and how they could hold out for as long as they needed. All they had to do was stick together like they had been doing all along. Virginia didn't think he was winning anyone over that had already decided to take flight, and look for a better place to go. He may have even tipped the scales to the leaving side for those who weren't sure if they wanted to stick it out or not. Virginia wasn't all that sure it was a good idea to stay now either. Then Doc opened it up to questions from the crowd, which, again, Virginia thought he had made another big mistake and rolled her eyes.

At first they were all yelling questions at once. Some were just yelling out profanities and pointing fingers at who they thought caused it. Then Charlie rose up and motioned everyone to be silent. They all grew quiet in anticipation of his words.

"Many of you here know me. You have known me for my entire life, knew my parents, and later you knew my sweet Annie. I am not going to stand up here and tell you that everything is going to be all right. I don't know if any of us will live through this or not. I know that there are more creatures out there than I can count. In some places, there are so many of them that you can hardly make out the landscape or any landmarks." Charlie took a deep breath then continued, "I spent my whole life trying to get away from this town. I wanted out of here so bad, there were times that I felt like I was going to burst if didn't leave. My Annie made me see just how special it was living here without all of the hustle and bustle of the big city. Looking back now, I think we survived because we were here—and not there."

Charlie looked around the room to make sure all eyes were on him now. The people on the stairway had even moved to the bottom, trying to hear him better. "All I am saying is this: if you want to leave, where will you go? Here, we have the school with heat and a water supply. Out there you have you, and your vehicle, and the creatures. Everywhere you stop you will have to look for them and deal with them, or move on quickly. Is that what we survived for? Did we survive just so we could run by day and cower in our cars by night? If we have to deal with the creatures; zombies, demons, or whatever you choose to call them, then let's do it here right now for our home!"

The crowd was starting to back Charlie up with more than a few yelling out 'You tell 'em Charlie' and 'Damn right brother!'

"For those of you that want to leave, I can't stop you. I will not even try to stop you. I will just wish you luck on your journey. Any man or woman that has a weapon and wants to fight for what we have, please meet me in the library parking lot in a half hour." Charlie walked off the stage and tried to make it to the stairs. The mood in the gymnasium was electrified with the excitement of people who had run far enough.

"I guess this means that we are fighting?" Albert asked Lori. Lori shrugged her shoulders and replied, "Virginia and I will fight, but I can't decide for you, Al."

"There is no decision, child. We are all family now, and we're staying with you and your sister," Zoe added before Albert could say anything.

"Damn straight pops!" added Jermaine.

"Then I guess we should start making our way out to the parking lot then. I only ask to be by Virginia and those dogs during the fighting," Albert replied with a smile.

Virginia wondered how many would stay and fight as she surveyed the room. When they arrived yesterday, a lot of the faces had looked like they were just waiting to die and be free of this new life. Now she could see life in a lot of those faces. There were still many she did not think could make it there or out on the open road. It was funny to her how easy she felt it was to decide who had it in them to live, and who did not.

Outside there were fifty or sixty people standing in the street between the school and library. Weapons amongst them ranged from handguns and rifles to large scissors and files. There was a man that Virginia didn't know standing on top of a metal barrel yelling something out to the crowd. From where she was at Virginia couldn't quite make out what he was saying. Whatever it was, the crowd up close was going nuts at every one of the man's pauses.

"There you guys are!" Todd ran toward them. "Mister, Doc says I should bring yous straight to the Library and not stop for any hot chocolate."

"We will follow you then," Lori replied as she motioned the rest of the group to follow.

Virginia and the lads fell in behind Todd as he cut a path through the crowd into the Library parking lot.

Inside they found Doc, Charlie, and a few men that Virginia didn't know.

"Welcome, please come in," Doc said. "Sit any place you like."

The room had a large conference table in the middle with the walls covered in book shelves.

Doc motioned over to Boo, who then stepped forward to the head of the table.

"We asked Todd to go find you guys because we have a big favor to ask. A few days ago, we created what we are calling the RCG, or Rivers Crossing Guard. We have between twenty or thirty people who volunteered."

"Sounds like a decent number for a beginning," Jermaine stated.

"True enough. We just have a few small problems, though. I don't think the majority of them have ever been in a fight; let alone fought those creatures out there," Boo added.

"How can that be? How can they still be alive and not have dealt with the zombies?" Lori asked shaking her head in amazement.

"Most of them hid or sought shelter in the school from the beginning," Charlie replied.

"What do you need from us, then?" Al asked.

"Boo and I are the only ones who have actually had any run in's with the creatures. Doc here has killed his fair share, but most of them were behind bars. None were coming at him without an obstruction between them. We need to make a group that can react to any breakthroughs," Charlie paused to gauge their reactions. "We think that you people would be perfect for that. Of course, Boo and I would also be part of it."

Lori looked over at Jermaine and Al, who nodded in agreement. Then before she could look at Virginia, she answered for them, "We are all in. Where do we start?"

"I don't want to hurt your feelings, but aren't you just a little young for this? You may feel more comfortable hanging with the others at the school," Doc offered to Virginia.

Before Virginia could voice an objection, Albert spoke up, "You may feel more comfortable with her hanging back at the school, and I am sure the folks over there would become very comfortable with her being there. I, for one, am more than comfortable with her and the dogs with us. If you have any notions of self-preservation, then she is with us."

Boo thought back to how he had seen the group calmly fighting against the onslaught of the creatures out on the road. Two people had stood out on that night apart from the others; one was the girl in question so he too spoke up, "The girl is as much a part of this unit as anyone else is. She stays!"

"Now that we have that settled, what exactly do you want us to do then?" Lori asked.

Boo walked over to the one wall that didn't have windows or shelving units on it and pulled down an old map of Rivers Crossing that had been hanging in the library since just after it had been built. Carefully placing it on the conference room table, Boo pulled a red felt tipped marker from his pocket and began drawing a red circle around the town. The circle started on the bridge they had crossed to enter town, followed the river to the raised train tracks, down past the school, around to what looked like a creek, and then back to the river.

"This is the area we had hoped to keep free of the creatures and in our control. It still is the primary goal at the moment," Boo said as he was pointing to the Main Street Bridge and the creek bridge. "We have a watch set up of three people each, on both bridges, taking eight hour shifts. They are armed and have a flare gun to alert us here if their bridge has been crossed by the creatures. In addition, we have another group taking eight hour shifts over along the train tracks on the other side of town." Boo paused and looked everyone over, "What we will do is try as best we can to plug any incursions."

"The six of us?" Albert asked.

"Well, I have a few other guys that are out showing the watchers what to do, so about ten of us," Boo replied. "The hope is that nothing gets past the circle, and we are all doing a whole lot of worrying for nothing."

CHAPTER 21

After the meeting ended, Lori took the others back to the RV while Virginia decided to take the lads out into the school yard. While they were in the library the snow had begun to fall, once again blanketing all of the ground in a fresh coat of fluffy snow. *It would be easy to see zombie tracks in this*, she thought to herself. Not that she needed the tracks with Zeus and Perseus and their keen sense of smell. The crowd was alive and very noisy; she thought that maybe deciding to fight back was bringing many of them back to life, if only for a little while.

"There you are, child!" A voice said from behind Virginia, she instantly recognized it as Zoe's.

"I have been looking all over for you!" Zoe stated exasperated.

"I was in the library with the others," Virginia replied.

"Making the war plans, I assume?"

"Something like that, I guess," Virginia replied with a forced smile.

"I am sure they have the best plan that they could come up with under our present circumstances," Zoe said looking off down Main Street. "Child, do you remember me telling you that we would need to keep an eye on Roy?"

Virginia remembered; it was the only reason that Roy was alive today. She had completely forgotten about Roy after they arrived at the school. He probably was doing his best to blend in with the survivors that were already here, rather than face the ones he had let down costing Joey his life.

"Old Roy took the last watch on the bridge we came in on about an hour ago."

Virginia could barely hide her surprise at the news. Roy was a coward in the worse way possible. Everyone in their group, including his wife, knew that Roy would sacrifice all others to save himself if it came down to that.

"Maybe the lads and I should go keep an eye on him," Virginia suggested, smiling at Zoe.

"I was thinking the exact same thing, child. Mind you, don't let him see you. Just make sure he is doing what he is supposed to be doing."

"If he does something else?" Virginia asked.

"Child, if he runs and hides again, you do what you feel needs done," Zoe replied looking down into the snow. She knew she had just told Virginia to end another human being's life because he was afraid. Most of the time, no, all of the time, Zoe would have protected someone like Roy as best she could. In this case, old Roy had already cost her great nephew his life and there could be no more.

Virginia understood what Zoe was saying, and knew the reasons behind it. Whistling to Zeus and Perseus, she led the dogs out the parking lot gate and up to the corner of Main Street. It felt good to be away from everyone again. It reminded her of being back at the bunker going on searches for zombies with the dogs. It was just her and the dogs back there, and in a small way it was what she wished for now. Things were much simpler then; she took care of Zeus and Perseus, they took care of her.

About a block away from the bridge Virginia picked out a house that would have an ideal view of the bridge and would get them out of the snow for a little while. It wouldn't be much warmer, but there would be no wind inside, and that would warm them up a bit.

Making her way off the street into a backyard, so as to not been seen by Roy, they cut through the yards until they made it to the front door of the house. Turning the handle and finding it to be unlocked, Virginia stepped aside and said to Zeus, "Ok boys, you know the drill. Go check it out for me." The lads stormed into the house, going in and out of every room until they were satisfied that no zombies were present. Once they returned to the living room and sat down, Virginia entered the house and locked the door behind her. She made her way through all of the lower rooms, just as the dogs had. It wasn't that she didn't trust them, Virginia was checking for any ways into the house that might be open. The last thing she wanted was to be concentrating on Roy and have something surprise them from behind. Not that Zeus would ever let that happen, she knew that, but being careful had kept her alive so far. Now was no time to quit.

Upstairs she found the master bedroom with a perfect view of the bridge. Stepping away from that momentarily she went in every bedroom and grabbed the blankets off the beds, bringing them back with her. Keeping an old quilt for herself, she made a large bed for the lads to lie on, and pulled out some bacon saved from breakfast. Splitting it up into three groups she gave the lads their share, "That has to hold you until we get back, so don't swallow it whole, Perseus," She chuckled looking at the lads enjoying their share before settling in to keep an eye on Roy.

On the far side of the bridge she could see that the herd was now gigantic in size, and inching close to the make-shift fence. Roy, on the other hand, was sitting in the tow truck running the motor. From the look of it, Roy was doing more drinking from a bottle than watching the bridge.

*****

The sound of the crowd could only be likened to that of a festival outside of the school. It carried over the raised train tracks like a hypnotic call to the zombies crossing the bridge. Earlier they had begun to mosey back off to wherever they had come from in search of food, but now the noise was calling them back and working them into a frenzy. What had been a few hundred less

255

than two hours ago, was now nearly four thousand creatures, pushing against each other and toward the stone wall of the raised tracks. As the pressure began to smash the creatures caught against the wall, they turned to the left and right to escape, causing a mass of decaying flesh to push against the van. At first the van held solid where Charlie had parked it, then it began to slide; a little at first, then a foot or so, until it created an opening that the creatures could see through. The visual way in caused the creatures to work up to a frenzy, and the van slid further, opening the gap wider through to the other side.

The first few zombies went unnoticed by the jubilant survivors, until the first person was taken down. The woman never saw death coming for her until she felt the teeth bite down into the back of her neck. At that point it was too late for her. Those standing near her had time to see her die before they too were brought down. The screaming and panic that followed worked the herd up even more and caused the survivors to panic. Where only a few minutes earlier they were giving their oaths to protect what they had and those who could not defend themselves, they were now running for the doors of the school. The elderly and young were being trampled by the very people they had been led to believe would protect them.

The first shots that were fired to help came from the roof of the school. In the lone gunman's state of fear, he wasn't picking out targets. Instead, he was firing a constant volley into the crowd hitting both humans and zombies indiscriminately. The major difference was that the humans went down to be eaten by the zombies that kept coming forward. Not until he ran out of ammo did his gun fall silent. Even then, he kept squeezing the trigger as if he had a full magazine loaded.

CHAPTER 22

The sounds of the rifle shots penetrated the library conference room where Doc, Charlie, and Boo were still going over safety plans. Boo ran to the window first and saw the melee of zombies and people trampling over the bright red snow. At first, a wave of fear washed through his body, but that was quickly replaced with disgust and anger. Grabbing his rifle off the side table, Boo smashed the window out and started picking his targets. First one zombie's head exploded, then another.

"What the hell!" Charlie screamed out when he reached the window.

"Charlie, take Doc and go through the tunnel! See if you can't help some of those people in, and then button her up tight."

Charlie forced himself back into reality and grabbed a petrified Doc by the shoulder, dragging him toward the door.

On the first floor they could see the carnage outside of the windows. Doc started to stop and bring his hands to his mouth, but

Charlie forced him on to the stairs leading to the basement. Once they reached the tunnel, Charlie took the lead, not knowing what they would find on the other end. It was dark and damp in there, but neither man stopped until they reached the door leading into the kitchen of the school. Charlie turned the handle slowly then kicked the door wide open to be greeted by Tressa aiming an old World War II forty-five at his face. Seeing Charlie, she dropped the pistol down to her side and said, "Thank God it's you two!"

"Are the creatures inside of the building?" asked Charlie.

"I don't think so," Tressa said. "There are a lot of us who got in, but I think even more are trapped outside."

Charlie nodded his head, "Doc, see if you can help Tressa out with the ones that made it back in." Making his way up the front stairway to the third floor, Charlie went into their room where he knew Boo had hidden some crates of dynamite under his bed. At the time, Charlie had thought it was an odd place to keep them, but that in a way, Boo was an odd old man to begin with and Charlie had never thought much of it after that. At the moment Charlie was incredibly grateful for that odd old man and his explosive packrat tendencies. Grabbing a crate, he headed up to the roof, finding Tim still squeezing off rounds from his empty gun.

"Tim! Give me a hand here!" Charlie ordered, forcing Tim to come back to reality.

Tim dropped his gun and grabbed the crate from Charlie, placing it on the ledge near where he had been standing a few minutes ago. Charlie handed Tim his rifle and said, "Make every shot count." Tim started firing indiscriminately again when he felt Charlie's hand on his shoulder, "Watch what old Boo is doing, Tim." He pointed over to the library window where Boo was shooting from; they could both see Boo picking his target out carefully, then firing, exploding the head of a zombie, taking the creature to the ground in a heap. "Pick your target, and hit only that target, and in the head."

Tim took a deep breath and picked a zombie out from the mass of bodies below them. Closing his eyes for a moment and taking a deep breath, Tim opened his eyes and selected his first target. With a thunderous boom, the gun fired as he squeezed the trigger, and the side of a zombie's head exploded. Looking over at Charlie Tim asked, "Like that, Charlie?" Charlie smiled back and lit the first stick of dynamite, then threw it has hard as he could toward the road.

*****

Lori heard the screams first and reacted by grabbing her crossbow and heading for the door. As hard as she tried, the mass of bodies pushing against the side of the RV was blocking the door, preventing her from opening it. Jermaine jumped up to join her in trying to force the door open, but it was useless. Outside all that they could see was a jumbled up mess of zombies and humans; too intertwined to get an accurate shot off. Just as Lori would line a zombie up, a human face would replace it. The last thing she wanted to do was help in the slaughter of fellow survivors.

As if by magic, the faces appearing zombies more and more. Only it wasn't any magic, the human numbers were growing fewer. Once targets became clearer, Lori started firing off arrows as fast as she could, and Jermaine forced the door of the RV open. Charging out, Jermaine began clubbing the nearest zombies until he was certain their heads had caved in. Albert, following behind, started toward the door to help the remaining survivors. With his right hand he was firing off shots at the zombies as he called out to Jermaine to help him reach the door. Once they had crossed in front of the RV, Lori started the motor and slid the gearshift into gear, cutting off the zombies that were now behind the guys. That was when an idea came to her. If she could use the RV to block the viaduct, they could possibly stem the flow into the area and retake the grounds.

Looking to her left to check on Jermaine and Al's progress, Lori pushed down on the gas pedal as she turned the wheel to the right. She would try to take as many out as possible on the way to the street. Up ahead she could see the steady stream entering through the narrow roadway. The crunch of the dead underneath the RV was nearly deafening as she again swung the vehicle to the right, out of the parking lot, and onto the street. The viaduct was narrow, but still left plenty of room on either side of the RV depending on how she drove into it. At the last moment, veering off to the left a little, and swinging hard back to the right, Lori caused the front of the RV to slam into the right side wall of the viaduct, throwing her out of her seat into the dashboard. A trickle of blood ran down into her left eye. She quickly wiped the blood away as she took a good look around. For now there would be no more zombies coming in by this route.

Outside the sound of gunfire had tripled in the last few moments. It was almost deafening when there was a knock on the door. Lori walked over and saw a smiling Boo standing there waving at her. Initially the door was jammed from the collision, but with Boo helping from the outside, it popped open.

"I wanted to make sure you were okay in there?"

Lori nodded her head that she was okay and grabbed her crossbow, handing Boo the extra quiver of arrows. "Do you think it will hold them?" she asked as she climbed down out of the RV.

"I think it will for now. Might give us enough time to concentrate on cleaning up the rest of the creatures before we have to worry about it."

Once outside, Lori saw an amazing sight. It was one she would have never even hazarded to guess could happen after the events only moments ago. Most of the survivors that had run for cover had returned armed and angry. They were weighing into the zombies with a vengeance now. Soon the ground was littered with the motionless dead corpses of the creatures and fallen survivors.

*****

When the shooting had started Virginia and the lads instinctively took defensive positions. Searching the street outside of the window, Virginia could see that there was no immediate danger to them where they were. Scanning the bridge brought a bigger and more pressing danger that would need to be acted on soon. Try as she might, there was no sign of Roy anywhere in Virginia's field of view.

"Come on lads, let's go take a look and see if we can find old Roy."

They left the house as cautiously as they had entered it. There was still no sign of the creatures other than the ones just across the bridge. There was still no sign of Roy either, for that matter.

"Zeus, Perseus, go find Roy." Virginia ordered the lads as they both took off to the other side of the street. Virginia decided to take a look in the cab of the tow truck just in case Roy had fallen asleep. It would be a small wonder that he hadn't with the amount of whiskey it looked like he was drinking. She could hear that the motor was still running as she made her way to the center of Main Street.

"What are you doing out here?" Roy demanded to know from the side of a mailbox on the corner.

"Roy, you're alright?" Virginia asked, wondering why he was so far from the truck and bridge.

"Of course I am. Why would you ask that? Perhaps you were hoping that I died in all that shooting going on up the street?"

"No Roy, I was doing a patrol and just happened to come by here," Virginia said, lying to Roy. "Whatever happened in the past, happened in the past. For now, we have to get that truck up against the bug, or we will have a big problem on our hands."

"I don't think that the truck will stop them. We have to get away from here as fast as we can," Roy stated with a tinge of fear cracking in his voice.

Not wanting to be confrontational, Virginia pleaded with Roy, "Then at the very least, fire the flare off Roy, so that they will know something's coming."

Roy raised the old Ruger revolver up and pointed it at Virginia, "Not so tough now are you? No dogs. No crossbow. You're just a mouthy little bitch!" Roy said as he motioned to where Virginia had laid her crossbow down in an attempt to make Roy feel safe. "What was it you said to me on the way here? That's right, I remember what it was now. You crawled up on top of me, like you were some kind of seductress, and whispered in my ear that when the time came you would kill me."

"Roy, I said that in a moment of anger and fear over losing a friend to the zombies," Virginia tried to explain.

Roy cocked the hammer on the Ruger and let out a deep breath, "It really doesn't matter now. They are probably all being eaten back there, and we are about to be overrun here. I just want to make this right in my own head before I die today." Taking aim at Virginia's head, Roy took another deep breath and started to squeeze the trigger when something plowed into him from the side with so much force that his breath was knocked out and he was brought to the ground. Zeus had come at a full run and leapt into the air and onto Roy. As they hit the ground Roy could feel Zeus's fangs clasping around his throat and he heard the Ruger discharge.

Zeus bit down with all the force he could muster and then shook his head from side to side. Once he had ripped a large section free from Roy's now lifeless body, Zeus turned toward Virginia who lay on the ground surrounded by bloodied snow.

Virginia felt the burning sensation emanating from her upper thigh on her left leg as she lay in the snow, trying to catch her breath. The night was now eerily silent all around them with the exception of the groans of the chain link fence on the bridge as it gave way.

Virginia reached into her coat's inside pocket and pulled out a knife that had belonged to Bob. He had given it to her in the early days, after Lori and she had joined him on the journey to a safer place. Cutting large strips of her undershirt to wrap around her leg, Virginia first cut a few smaller ones from the strips and forced one down into the bullet hole. She then repeated the process where the bullet had exited her leg in the back. Not knowing if it would help or hurt, Virginia thought it might possibly help stop the bleeding. Then she used the rest of the strips to tie around the leg, keeping the smaller strips in.

Laying back into the cold wet snow to rest for a few minutes, Virginia started to doze off. It was only Perseus's cold, wet tongue, licking her face that stopped the slide into slumber. The sounds of the chain link fence giving way on the bridge convinced her that they needed to get moving toward the school or a safer place to hold up. Calling Zeus over to Perseus, she tried to use them to climb off the ground. The pain coming from her leg was excruciating, and she slumped back down, hard. Zeus walked over her and stood facing the bridge. He growled at the growing numbers of the herd now moving toward the middle.

Virginia crawled through the bloody snow over to her crossbow and quiver. Through the pain, she sat up and looked at the lads, then beyond them. For now, the herd was not paying any attention to them. They poured across the bridge and were beginning to fan out. Virginia didn't know how long they could hope to go unnoticed, but she figured it was time to try and move. Seeing the street sign and mailbox on the corner, she decided to crawl over to it and try to use one of them to stand. If she could stand, she would then figure out how she could move without attracting any attention. The one thing she had noticed was that these zombies were not moving slowly, without purpose. The creatures seemed to be checking out the area just this side of the bridge. If they were two-point-zeros, Virginia didn't hold out much hope on making it away from there. Pushing the snow from in front of her, she inched her way painfully toward the mailbox. All the while Perseus walked besides her, and Zeus stayed about ten feet away watching the bridge. As she advanced, the old dog would move to a new position that he felt was a good place to cover his human friend.

Once she reached the street sign and mailbox, Virginia tried as hard as she could to stand up. Even Perseus had grabbed a hold of the back of her coat, in an attempt to help her stand, but it was of no use. While there was a slim chance of standing in the now deep snow, there was no way that Virginia could see herself walking out of there.

"Ok Lads, I think it is time for you to go now," Virginia said as she stuck several arrows into the snow where she could easily reach them. Perseus lay his head across her ankles and let out a whimper. "I mean it; you two have to go! There is no reason that I can see that would say we all need to die here today!"

Zeus walked over and lay down next to Virginia, putting his ears flat back. He was still keeping an eye on the advancing herd, but pushed his body up against Virginia's. It was his way of telling her that he would not leave this place without her, and neither would Perseus.

Once Virginia was happy with the number of arrows placed around her, she took the quiver and tied it to the street pole. It was her hope that it would not move too much as she reached for the remaining arrows. Uncertain how long she could hold out, or how many would be taken with her, Virginia decided that it was as good a place as any to make her stand. With each hand she petted her only friends in the world and thought about being back home with Mom, Dad, and Lori. After a good snow like this, she would just now be coming in for dinner and would be fielding questions if she had seen her brother outside anywhere. Her dad would go to the door again and yell her brother's name two or three times followed by, "I don't know where the hell that boy gets off to!" Virginia had not been able to remember them since all of this had begun; it brought a smile to her face.

Bending over and wrapping her arms around Zeus' neck, she hugged him long and hard, only stopping when Perseus began licking her cheek again. "Of course I haven't forgotten you, boy," Virginia reassured him as she hugged him next. Zeus's growl brought her attention back to the impending surge of zombies that was close to overtaking their position. Virginia pulled an arrow from the now bloody snow and fixed it into the crossbow. "Remember boys, if it gets too bad, you get out of here and go find Lori." Taking aim, Virginia sighted one about two hundred yards from where she was. With a slight squeeze of the trigger the arrow was let loose and on its way to the mark she had picked. With a quiet thump, cushioned by the snow, it found its home dead center of the creature's left eye. Falling to the ground, it was barely noticed by the herd around it.

CHAPTER 23

Tressa had come outside just as the first screams were heard at the viaduct.

Immediately, she found Todd, who was working himself into a complete breakdown at the thought of the zombies getting him. Having grown accustomed to calming her uncle down over the past few months, she started to bring him back to reality.

"Settle down, Todd. Please. We have to stay calm if we want everything to be okay and get to a safe spot, right?"

Todd had tears sliding down his cheeks as he tried to breathe deep like Tressa had taught him to do when he was scared.

"I want you to run over to the door, and then go straight to the kitchen and wait for me," Tressa said, trying to get Todd to focus on her words. Experience had proven that Todd followed orders better when he was petrified with fear than with reasoning.

"Todd, did you hear what I just said?!"

Todd shook his head up and down 'yes'. "You said I should go inside and wait for you in the kitchen, behind the locker door," Todd replied between sobs as the tears started to fall more steadily. Tressa didn't say anything about the metal food locker, but thought better of correcting

Todd. If that would make him move, and he felt safer, then she was ok with it. "Now get moving Todd, before they get over here!"

Todd didn't even stop to think about Tressa's safety as he took off at full speed toward the front door. Tressa wasn't for sure, but it looked like Todd may have knocked a few other men off their feet as he ran. Unfortunately, when he got to the door there was no way for him to get in. The survivors had the door blocked as everyone tried to get inside at the same time. One lady even turned to Todd and screamed at him, "Women and children first, you oversized jackass!" Todd was shocked at the mean lady's use of such a word. He turned around and started marching off to find Tressa. He had to tell her what the mean lady had said to him, knowing full well that Tressa would put her in her place as soon as she found out. He didn't find Tressa because the zombies had crossed into the school yard now, slaughtering all that they could catch. The only thing that he could remember once he saw them was Tressa telling him to run and get into the school where it was safe. Only there was no way for him to get into the school, so Todd took the next best route that he could see. Todd began sprinting toward Main Street and the steps that led down from the schoolyard onto the street. There were no zombies this way which made him, at least for a little while, feel safer. Once he made it to the street, Todd didn't pause for a breath, he just kept running as hard as he possibly could. He ran until there was nothing around him but an empty street and houses along it. The sounds of gunfire behind him forced him to start running again. When he noticed a stairwell behind one of the Victorian houses, Todd ran there to hide. Trying to catch his breath, Todd tried in vain to remember what Tressa had told him. Now he wasn't even sure if Tressa got away from the zombies like he had. This worry made him start crying at the possibility of having lost Tressa, and the prospect of being alone for the first time in his life.

Todd heard a single gunshot come from up the street in the other direction. Slowly lifting his head above the top of the stairwell and looking in all directions, he listened. There was nothing but silence now, and that scared him even more. Climbing up to ground level on shaky legs, he came out of the stairwell and started in the direction the shot had come from. If it was only one shot, Todd thought, maybe it was a sign from Tressa that he should follow it back to her.

At the curb by the street, he listened for any other sounds. There was no gun fire, no screams or cries for help that he could hear. He thought maybe it was safe now; the zombies had all gone back where they had come from. As he looked around he thought he saw the puppies way up the street by the corner. The puppies meant safety to Todd, so he broke into a mad dash to get to them before they left him all alone again.

Getting closer, Todd saw a third figure was laying in the snow kind of behind the mailbox. Tressa had always told Todd never to play close to the street; Todd never did after that. In his mind he could not understand why someone would want to lay by the street. *It was much too close and a car could hit you or something,* he thought to himself.

Perseus had seen Todd first, and stood, leaving to greet him about twenty yards away from Virginia. Todd fell on the ground and was rolling around in the snow trying to play with him. Perseus kept grabbing a hold of his sleeve, trying to pull him toward Virginia when Zeus let out a little bark. Todd stopped laughing and looked up at Zeus, and that was when he noticed that the girl was hurt. *That was why she was laying so close to the road,* he thought.

"OH NO! You're hurt; how did this happen?" Todd screamed as he ran toward Virginia and then slid thru the snow until he stopped right next to her. Zeus let out a low mean growl as Todd had drawn the attention of the herd, which was now heading toward them in earnest.

"Todd, can you help me get out of here?" Virginia asked without looking at him. She had sighted another zombie and fired an arrow at it.

"Todd can help you! I am strong for my little size," Todd said as he roughly picked her up and started to throw her over his left shoulder. Virginia cried out in pain as she clinched her teeth together, "Easy, Todd, that hurts a lot." Then Virginia pointed at the quiver, "We need the arrows too, Todd." Todd reached down and tugged on the quiver. At first it didn't budge, so he pulled with a little more force until the strap ripped apart. "Got the arrows. Now can we go?"

"Yes, Todd. Please run as fast as you can to the school."

Todd froze in place as Virginia could hear the zombies growing closer to them, "Todd, we have to go now!"

"Tressa told me to run *from* the school, because the creatures were there," Todd whispered to her as he started crying again.

"Todd, run to the school and we will see if we need to run someplace else, okay? The lads will not let us go there if there are any zombies around."

Todd nodded his head and wiped his eyes before he started running again with everything he had, back to where he had started from. Todd wasn't as afraid as before because he had Virginia with him, and she was tougher than even Tressa was. Plus, the puppy in front of him was clearing all the bad things out of the way while the big puppy behind him was stopping those same bad things from catching him.

Virginia tried as best as she could to keep her head lifted up. Todd had thrown her over his shoulder like she was a sack of potatoes, and with him running, she was being bounced all over the place. A few times she had almost dropped the crossbow and arrow on the ground. Only luck had allowed her to keep a decent grip on it through all the jostling. Virginia resigned herself to the fact that her only easy view would be of Todd's backside and the passing street below her, until a horrifying squeal came from behind them. Raising her head, she saw Zeus being surrounded by zombies, and for an instant, she thought she had seen him go down.

"TODD! STOP RIGHT NOW!" Virginia screamed as she raised the crossbow up and fired at one of the zombies. Todd slid to a stop, nearly falling as the arrow found its mark, felling the creature. The opening allowed her to see Zeus in the middle of them, fighting with everything he had to break free. "Perseus, help Zeus!" Virginia ordered as she saw the black flash of the other dog charge into the fight. "Todd, I need the arrows!"

Todd handed her three arrows from the quiver, and Virginia started picking off more zombies. For now they were in luck, as Zeus had taken on the vanguard of the herd. If she could pick enough off, he could get out of there and head to safety alongside her and Todd.

Once Perseus made it to Zeus's side the battle seemed to be tilting in their favor. While one dog was worthwhile to take on, the remaining zombies started to back away from two. Virginia kept picking them off as fast as she could until Todd said, "There are no more arrows Missus." Virginia let her head drop and then called the lads to come to her. Perseus ran as fast as ever, but Zeus was moving slow and labored. Not sure if he could make it or not in his condition, Virginia told Todd, "Why don't you put me down over there by Zeus, and then you and Perseus get out of here?"

Todd stamped his large foot into the snow and replied, "Then Todd and the puppy would be alone again! I don't want to be alone again out here!"

"Todd, Zeus doesn't look like he can run, and I can't leave him by himself. Please, just leave me by Zeus so I can be with him if this is the end for the two of us. I can't leave him behind, do you understand?" Virginia was now crying in a way that she had not cried since the day the authorities came to take her mother to the quarantine center. Todd stamped his feet again and said no as Virginia began beating his back with the crossbow.

"Todd will carry the puppy *and* you!" He yelled as he ran forward to get Zeus.

"You can't carry us both! Zeus weighs over one hundred and seventy pounds, Todd. All you will do is get us all eaten."

Todd wasn't hearing anything that she was saying. He ran as hard as he could until he got to Zeus. First he reached down, nearly dropping Virginia, and pulled as many arrows out from the corpses that he could while Perseus kept what was left of the vanguard at bay. Then after handing each and every one to Virginia, he looked at Zeus and said, "Come here, big fella, and let me give you a ride home." Zeus looked at Todd cautiously, and then as if he understood what Todd was saying, he jumped up into Todd's waiting arm. After wrapping it around the puppy, Todd turned and ran like he had never run before. Much faster than he had run from the school, and even faster when Perseus took the lead again to show him the way home to Tressa.

Behind them, the herd was on the move following them. Virginia had never seen anything other than the two-point-zeros move this fast. With how much she was being bounced around by Todd, she would strain to look up and see how far off they were. Unfortunately, with every look they were closer and gaining on them. *There is no hope of outrunning them like this,* Virginia thought to herself. There wasn't even a way for her to fire at the ones growing uncomfortably close behind. At a few points, Virginia felt that she could clearly read the "Cubs" logo on the shirt that one was wearing, but then Todd would bounce her so hard her head would slam into his back. As far as Todd was concerned, he felt that they were halfway to the school and Tressa. When he saw his foot prints leading off the street into the stairwell he almost lost his footing looking for it.

"Todd, are you ok?" Virginia asked as he slid and almost fell.

In a hoarse, out of breath voice, Todd replied, "Okay, for now….have to keep running…."

Virginia saw Perseus turn and run toward the herd, "Perseus, NO! Lead!"

Hearing Virginia, Perseus stopped and snarled at the zombies, then turned to take his place back in the lead. She was angry at his trying to hold off the herd, but

Perseus *did* throw them off of their stride and allowed Todd to gain a few steps ahead of them. When they hit a patch of road that had tire ruts under the fresh snow, it helped to slow the herd down even more. Virginia was glad to see that zombies couldn't just adapt to sudden changes around them. It gave Todd a decent lead to stay out in front now. Hope was returning to her slowly. As hard as it was for her to believe, Todd was about to save the day. Forcing herself to smile at their good fortune, Virginia patted Todd on the back and said, "Run like the wind, Todd! Run like the wind."

Todd let out a "Yippee" as best he could. Being so out of breath, Todd felt that he was ready to faint. That was when Todd's left foot hit a patch of ice and he lost his footing. All three of them hit the ground hard with Todd underneath the pile. He looked up and started crying because of the pain in his back and chest. Fighting to get up with Virginia and Zeus still wrapped inside of his arms while his chest ached for air, Todd could see the library was only two or three buildings away from them. "School and library," Todd said, trying to point down the street.

"Todd, I need you to help me walk. Can you do that, Todd?" Virginia asked as she rolled out of Todd's grasp. "Zeus, go to the school. Go get Lori." Zeus got to his feet and slowly started heading to the school while Perseus took up a defensive position next to Virginia. "Okay Todd, get up and help me up. Get on this side of me and help me walk without putting weight on my leg." Todd did as he was told until he saw how close the zombies were to them now. Every fiber of his being wanted to cry and run as fast as he could; only he wouldn't leave Virginia now, no matter what happened. She was his only friend besides Tressa.

They made it about ten feet before the first zombie reached them. Perseus took it down, but he didn't kill the creature so it crawled toward them until the next zombie passed it by. Virginia shifted and shot it in the head. Reloading as they took a few more steps, she shifted and repeated the process again. Soon there were too many for her and Perseus to fight, so she ordered Perseus to guard Zeus, who had returned, appearing to have caught his second wind. Instead of Perseus joining him, it was Zeus that came to the rescue. Something hit Todd hard and he fell, pulling Virginia to the ground with him. The sky went from a hazy grey with heavy snow falling, to a dark mass of smelly dead faces closing in on them.

For a while, Zeus and Perseus kept the zombies at a distance from Virginia. The circle around them began to close in tighter and tighter, until there was no daylight left to be seen. The only sounds were the awful moaning murmurs of the zombies, punctuated by the lads' snarling and teeth snapping together. Virginia closed her eyes and thought about her family and Bob. In her mind, she had done her best to survive in this world that was left to them. If not her father, she was sure that Bob would have been very proud of her and the lads. Sleep was coming on fast for her, *probably from the loss of blood*, Virginia thought. It didn't really matter to her now, did it? Not much point in figuring it out just before she was going to die.

CHAPTER 24

Charlie and Tim scanned the corpses from the roof of the school using high powered rifles with scopes. Any movement and either man would have placed a bullet square into the zombies head. Below, others were walking through the carnage checking for survivors and verifying that the zombies were dead.

"Tim, keep a good eye on the RV, too. I am going to check the front," Charlie said as he walked through the snow toward Main Street.

"Gotcha, boss," Tim confirmed.

There were fewer bodies in front of the school, but still more than expected. Wiping the snow from the ledge and then using it to rest the rifle on, Charlie started slowly scanning the corpses for movement. Of the fallen, a few of the faces looked familiar, but he couldn't remember if he knew their names or not.

Sudden movement coming down Main Street in his peripheral vision caught Charlie's attention. Swinging the rifle over and looking through the scope, he saw the massive herd coming toward them. A few yards from the front, there was what looked like the two dogs and the girl that had just come to the school; lying in the snow nearby was the big guy, Todd. Charlie ran over to where Tim was and grabbed the backpack laying nearby in the snow. Pulling the flare gun out with two flares, Charlie fired the first toward the herd.

"Tim, go to the front and try to keep the creatures off the people in the street as best you can!" Charlie ordered as he headed toward the door, grabbing a few sticks of dynamite as he passed. Once he was out on the schoolyard, Charlie caught sight of Boo and Lori, and he began franticly waving his hand.

"Charlie, what is wrong? You look like you just saw a ghost," Boo said.

"There is a whole shitload of the creatures coming down Main Street. That isn't the worst of it; the girl and the dogs are lying in their path between us and them."

Lori lost all color in her face and sprinted toward Main Street. Jermaine and Al followed, trying desperately to catch up. Once on Main Street, Lori saw the group lying directly in front of the herd. Again the three broke into a full run toward Virginia. Just past the library, Lori's little sister faded from view. The zombies now had them surrounded, and were closing in. Luckily Lori and the others were still unnoticed and had the element of surprise on their side.

The first volley of gunfire and explosions had little effect on Lori. Her focus was completely on reaching Virginia and pulling her out of there safely, if possible. The closer Lori got the more the feeling came over her that all was lost and hopeless; despite that her body felt stronger and impervious to pain or feeling. There was no way of knowing why or how she could be feeling both at a time. Before her the creatures were falling in ever larger numbers. The gunfire was no longer in volleys, but a constant echo of gun blasts broken only by the sound of large, concentrated explosions. Off to the left a whooshing sound cut through the noise and fires erupted in several of the houses. People were coming up the street to join in the rescue.

Finally reaching Virginia, Lori reached down for her bow and shoved the end into the head of a large zombie. She then jumped onto the back of the next one, sinking her teeth into the neck while reaching around to rip out its throat. In her mind it was her and the zombies alone. There was no reason to be found in her actions; there was only death and destruction. Strength that Lori had never known came to her as she worked her way through them, hissing and growling. Once she made it to Virginia and Todd, she whirled around at the herd, picking the largest one that she could find. Springing like a tigress, she was on it, sinking what she would later think were fangs into its neck. The creature tried to break free of the death grip Lori had on it, but could not. There was a sudden blast close to her ear and the zombie's head exploded, taking her quarry down. Landing on top, she jumped up and onto the next target. Over and over, the instinct to kill led Lori through the maze of zombies surrounding them. After a while she didn't even hear the ruckus around her. She saw the creatures and she killed them where they stood.

Al tried to keep up with Lori as best as his old legs would allow, but he settled for standing guard over Virginia and Zeus. Anything that got passed Lori had to make it through Jermaine, and then Al. For the first time, there was no hint of fear within him. *There is no time to be afraid*, he thought to himself. Everything moved in slow motion. Each shot he fired hit its mark, and with machine precision, the next was lined up. Then, seeing Lori off in the distance, fear returned to Al for just an instant, but long enough. Al began to notice that Lori looked more like the zombies they were fighting than she looked like herself. Her skin was gray and sallow; Albert could swear on his mother's soul that he saw the glint of fangs in the remaining light. Al closed his eyes and shook his head in a desperate attempt to rid himself of the vision.

Al didn't see the creature get past Jermaine; charging with speed, toward him. The last thing on earth that Albert saw was the contorted, half decayed face of a zombie as it reached into his chest, breaking all of his ribs. The creature bit down on Al's face as it pulled his still beating heart out. As Al fell to the ground the first of three shots hit the creature, causing it to twitch with each strike. Regaining its footing, the creature took Al's heart and walked off toward the bridge. The zombies were all walking away.

No one had ever seen the creatures break off an attack before.

Lori fell to the ground, exhausted, barely able to breathe. She felt as if her body was on fire and about to explode any minute.

"Umm, are you okay?" Jermaine asked.

Turning her face away, because she wasn't sure exactly what she looked like and feared that she may look like a zombie, Lori replied, "I am fine. Virginia?"

"I think she will live. Deep down I think she has a mean side that will not let her be anything but fine," Jermaine said kneeling down beside Lori. "We lost Al, though. I think one got passed me."

Charlie and Boo made their way over to Lori and fell to the ground. It was easy to see that Boo had suffered some pretty bad wounds during the fight, but Charlie looked like he was okay.

No one said anything for a few minutes while the three stared at Lori. Seeing is believing, except the three were seeing something that their minds refused to believe. All around them people were moving through the corpses; congratulating each other on a great victory. Most felt it would be a turning point in the human existence on earth. Doc was leading a group of men from one corpse to another, looking for wounded. When he made it to their group, Doc kneeled down and started checking Virginia's leg.

"Looks like you're going to make it, young lady," Doc said with a smile.

Moving over to Albert, Doc closed his eyes and whispered something into his ear. Rising and moving over to Boo, he knelt down again.

"I am doing well, Doc. Why don't you go help someone that needs it?"

"Beau, I do believe someone has shot you. Do the creatures carry guns now?" Doc asked smiling.

"No, they do not!" Boo replied. "I think one of ours got a little excited and started shooting anything that moved. I heard someone yell sorry right after I got hit!"

Turning to one of the men that followed him Doc motioned, "Take these three to the main floor of the library.

Someone stay with them while the rest of you go grab some cots. I will be along in a little while to check on them."

With that Doc continued on his way checking the wounded.

Lori stood up and reached a hand down to Charlie. Looking up into her eyes, Charlie couldn't believe how beautiful they were now after seeing what he had seen moments ago. Charlie was unsure at first if he should grab the hand being offered. Jermaine interrupted his contemplation, "Look, what you fellas saw a little while ago isn't anything. I trust my life in this woman's hands now just like I did before we got here."

Everyone could hear the defensive nature that Jermaine's tone had taken.

Charlie reached up and took the hand being offered. As far as he could tell this whole battle may have turned out a lot different had Lori not charged into the herd the way she did.

"I have been in battles all across the South Pacific, said prayers to the All Mighty in a foxhole that I shared with an atheist; I have seen all natures of evil back in those days. Cost me my wife and boys when I came home as I will forever be stuck in those places...what I saw today is no different than what I saw back then," Boo said.

"You actually pray? Know the words to a prayer?" Charlie asked jokingly.

"Yes, I do. And I sure as hell did that night. Funny thing is, my atheist friend was pretty good at praying by morning, too."

The men went over to Virginia and gently picked her up. Breathing normally but exhausted, she said nothing until they started to move toward the library, "Are Todd and Zeus ok?"

Todd was curled up in a ball where he had first hit the ground covered in blood. Next to him lay Zeus and Perseus, as if they were standing guard over their new friend.

"Looks like they're fine to me," Lori replied. "Todd, do you want to go with Virginia and make sure she gets to the library?"

Todd jumped up on his feet, "Really? Can I go too? Can I look for Tressa after we get in the library?"

One of the men chuckled and replied, "Tressa is busy making food for all of these brave people. You can go see her in the kitchen if you want, Todd."

"I better make sure Virginia and the puppies are okay first, Mister."

Todd reached down and petted the lads, then followed the men carrying Boo and Virginia.

Two men walked alongside Lori until Charlie and Jermaine politely pushed them away from her, taking their place. Neither of them liked the way those two were acting toward someone that they personally thought was a hero. Lori was quite possibly the only reason they were all walking and talking right now. Charlie made a mental note to talk to Doc about it.

CHAPTER 25

The back half of the main floor of the library had been turned into a make-shift triage center. The wounded went there first then would move to either the rooms on the upper floor, or be carried out the side entrance to a waiting van. No one talked about where they were being taken to, or why. Whenever it was brought up to Doc or Aunt Zoe they would skirt the subject and start talking about the patient's own issues. Virginia noticed that Charlie was stopping by to see Lori on an almost routine schedule. Not knowing how long they had been in the library frustrated her, but it soon passed. On one of the visits Charlie brought along what Virginia thought were the ugliest plastic flowers that she had ever seen. When Lori questioned him as to where he had found the plastic roses, Charlie simply said, "Old lady Grabitz never could grow anything, so she surrounded her home with plastic flowers. If you asked her, she would tell you that she was the only one with beautiful flowers during the droughts."

Thinking that maybe something was happening between the two made Virginia happy. She liked seeing how Lori lit up every time he visited. She was so happy with the ugly, fake flowers. It had been a long time since Virginia saw her glow like this. It was hard to believe that she did, after what everyone saw that day. Lori's secret and knowledge of what was inside of her was out. No one acted strange, they all acted as though they had not seen anything; or so Virginia had thought.

That day, when Doc made his rounds, Charlie asked him, "Why is Lori still in the library? When is she going to be free to go back to the dorm?"

Doc sighed, "Charlie, first of all, I am not sure she can return to our room with the way you are carrying on. Secondly, we have a few things to talk about before Lori is free to go back over to the school. On the other hand, Virginia is getting around here pretty well; she could possibly go by next weekend."

"Doc, I don't see a reason for either to be in here. Boo was wounded just as bad as the girl and he is back at the school," Charlie replied.

Doc looked around at the other patients in the room, then reached for the crutches near Virginia, "Come on, then. I think it is time we have a talk."

Doc led them into a side room that had been used in years long passed for Saturday afternoon readings to the children. He motioned for everyone to sit. He helped Virginia into a chair and closed the door. Doc took in a deep breath while he searched for the words to say, just as he had done so many times in the past when preparing to give bad news.

"Everyone here thinks Lori is a hero. In fact, they are having a celebration dinner with games for the kids this coming Saturday."

"Then she should be allowed to be there; if it is a celebration in her honor," Charlie replied.

"Well, it isn't *just* in her honor, Charlie. A lot of people had a hand in the outcome of that day: Todd, Virginia, you, and countless others."

"We all did our part, Doc, but if she didn't block the viaduct, or charge into the herd to save Virginia, nothing would be here now and you know that. Or perhaps you don't know that, because I don't remember seeing *you* fight the creatures!" Charlie stated.

Doc tried to pat Charlie's shoulder but was brushed away. He turned toward Lori, "I don't know what happened to you out there. I don't know if you're turning into one of those creatures or if, inside of you, you hold the secret to turning them back. I *do* know that other than the few who fought alongside of you, you scare a lot of the people here now. They think one night you will wake up as a creature and kill as many as you can. And you demonstrated you'd do a good job of it." Looking over at Virginia, Doc continued, "*You* have scared the hell out of them since day one. How does a girl of fourteen or fifteen get so good at killing?"

Before either could reply, Charlie asked, "So they are doomed to live in the library forever? Or...?"

"Don't be silly, Charlie. The library couldn't hold or keep anyone in that didn't want to stay here. Even now there would be no way for us to keep them in here. I wanted to move Lori over to the jail, but Beau said he would take down any man that tried to move either girl out of the library. Funny thing is, all you kids gave him the name Boo because he scared you, and now as an old man, he still does."

"So what are our options?" Lori asked.

"The best I can come up with is for you two to leave. Follow that map of yours, and try to find a safe place to hold out until the world decides to right itself."

Charlie stood up and faced Doc, looking him squarely in the eyes, "What the hell are you talking about, Doc? That is not what you said this place would be!"

Not budging an inch, Doc replied, "Then maybe you should step up and lead, Charlie, because after that day these people feel they have something here worth protecting, and they will protect it. I can't promise you how long I can hold them back, or even how long their fear of what Beau will do will stop them, but most of the ones that survived are not from Rivers Crossing; they don't have the same feelings for what we set out to do. They are looking to survive and rebuild what we all had before this."

"So to do that, we kill innocents? Boot them out of here and let them fend for themselves?"

Doc sat back down, "I think that these two could take care of themselves just like they did before getting here, Charlie."

Charlie too sat back down, "Then it is settled, isn't it? The three of us will leave as soon as I can get some supplies together."

"Aww, come on, Charlie! No one says *you* have to go!" Doc exclaimed.

"Virginia and I will be fine by ourselves, Charlie. You don't have to leave your home," Lori added.

"Doc, I have said since the beginning that as soon as you got things going here, I was leaving. Well, you have things going somewhat, and I don't much like what I see around here anymore!" Charlie added.

Doc knew the look on Charlie's face well enough to know that no amount of reasoning would change his mind. "Charlie, we have tried hard to make the people here feel like they are part of the community. It is the only way we can start rebuilding some kind of normal life here."

"Understood Doc, and I wish you the best of luck with that," Charlie replied.

"Nothing will change your mind?"

Charlie took a long look at Virginia, and then into Lori's eyes, "I don't think so, Doc."

Doc dug deep into his coat pocket and pulled out a worn out, old Chicago Bears key chain with two keys dangling from it. "Outside, you will find a black Chevy Suburban with a full tank of gas. Tim and Tom went over to your old house and went through it room by room. They have assured me that it is safe to stay in. Thought maybe the ladies here would be a little more comfortable there; if you're all right with that, Charlie."

Charlie smiled at Doc, "That would be fine, my old friend. Thank you, Doc."

Doc stood up and walked over to Charlie, handing him the keys, and surprised Charlie by enveloping him in a bear hug, "You take care out there, Charles. I have always thought about you as if you were the son I never had."

Breaking away, Charlie could see that Doc had a tear rolling down his cheek as he said good-bye to the girls and left.

Charlie looked over at Lori and said, "Well, are you two ready to get out of here?"

Out on the street they found the black suburban waiting for them, just as Doc said. Virginia was on edge; there was no way of knowing what kind of reception they would get from anyone they might run into.

The first person they saw came up and gave Lori and Virginia a big hug and said thank you. Others watched with cautious eyes on the freaks, or at least Virginia thought that was what they were thinking. She had no way of really knowing, short of asking; but that didn't seem like a good idea right now.

Once she was in the suburban with Zeus and Perseus sitting on the bench seat next to her, Virginia could see a thick smoke. Looking around she could see where the smoke was coming from. She vaguely remembered the houses exploding, but that wasn't the source. There was a mound of bodies in the middle of the street. It was burning. The smoke was thick and black, carrying the stench of burning flesh with it. They drove past it as if it was some kind of road construction placed in their way to hinder the trip.

Reaching Charlie's street, they drove down a few houses to where there were a few other cars and a new Winnebago. After pulling into the little room that was left in the driveway, they noticed waiting on the porch for them were Jermaine, Boo and Zoe.

"Everything is all loaded and ready for us to hit the road," Jermaine said as he hugged Lori, and then Virginia.

"You are all coming?" Virginia asked.

"Everyone but me, child," replied Zoe. "I am getting too old to go off wandering the open road, especially now that my nephew and great nephew are gone."

"Boo, thank you for coming to say goodbye. I was planning on going back over to the school, after we got settled in here, to find you," Charlie said.

Boo shook his head and laughed at Charlie, "I wouldn't be able to live with myself if something happened to you. Someone has to come and keep you from going off on halfcocked missions to save damsels in distress." Then turning to Lori, he added, "I have been looking over Bob's map. I like the way he thinks; I agree with his route until you get down by Atlanta. We may want to avoid the bigger cities all together."

"We can all talk about that on the road," Lori replied. "When are we planning on leaving?"

"We have everything loaded and ready to go. Boo and I took everything out of the old RV and loaded it into the new one," Jermaine replied.

"It's nine-thirty, if we leave now we should be in Clarksville by two, two-thirty. There are a few places that I would like to pick up some more ammo, if they still have it," Boo stated.

Zoe hugged Virginia and Lori goodbye, and then hugged Jermaine, "I am trusting you; make sure my girls are always safe."

Jermaine nodded.

Charlie drove the suburban out, leading the new RV and Boo in a Ford four-by-four. Virginia wasn't sure where he had found it, nor did she know where they had found a new RV.

Their brief stay at the school had taught Virginia that she could love and care for people again. Still, it was nice to be back on the road following Bob's map. It made her feel as if Bob was still with them, and, in a way, he *was* still with her in the actions that she took every day. Zoe had given her a note from Doc, for Lori and her to read once they were on the road, far from Rivers Crossing. Along with the note Doc had given them meds for Virginia and Boo to take until they were finished healing. Having taken a few pain pills just before they said their final goodbyes, Virginia could feel sleep closing in on her fast. The doubts that she had over the new Lori were no longer as strong as before. Even the lads didn't seem to act as if Lori could possibly be a danger to anyone. The last thing Virginia would see before drifting off to sleep was the vast, empty, white landscape.

"Looks like Virginia and the dogs are out like a light," Jermaine said.

"Good, I think she needed it. She wasn't sleeping very well in the library, at all," Lori replied. After a few minutes of silence, she added, "Jermaine, can I ask why you would want to keep traveling with us after…"

"I think we all knew something was different about you all along. There is definitely something different about Virginia," he replied, laughing.

"I know, but now that you know what the different part is about me... that doesn't worry you?"

"Back there, that old Doctor said that you were the future of the human race; sort of a hybrid-human, or that you carried the cure. Either way, I am part of this group and not that one." Jermaine replied, looking out over the white fields. "Besides, I think someone has a crush on you, and I would be remiss in my duties if I wasn't here to chaperone"

"Crush on me? How old do you think I am?"

"You can have a crush at any age," Jermaine replied. "I am going to catch some shut eye. Wake me up when you want me to drive."

"I think I can make it into Clarksville; you can take it from there."

The thought had never occurred to Lori that Charlie had a crush on her. He was nice, and even nicer to *her*, bringing those stupid, ugly, fake roses that he had picked for her. Okay, she admitted to herself, she didn't think they were quite so ugly or so stupid when she thought more about it. It was a nice thought, and it made her feel special in a way that she had never known before. In a small way she could see herself with Charlie; even if you discounted the fact that pickings were slim in the world that they lived in now. *Only time will tell*, she thought to herself, as she proceeded driving down the highway.

They weren't far from Rivers Crossing when Lori maneuvered sharply to bring the RV to a sudden stop behind Charlie. Fear grasped her throat while laboring to breathe. She wondered to herself if they had run into the herd. Charlie was outside of the Suburban waving her to come forward with a big grin, as if he had just won the lottery. On weakening legs Lori ignored the minor rumblings of Jermain and Virginia as she got out and went to Charlie. Once there she noticed Charlie pointing up the road, off to the left, just above the ditch.

"It can't be...." Lori said.

"I think it can be and is Walter." Charlie replied.

Her legs growing stronger, Lori broke into a jog bordering on a sprint, toward the child with Charlie close behind.

"Walter, it is you!"

Water turned to face Lori and they could see the dried blood on his face. In any other time, Walter would have looked like he had just eaten the family's cherry pie with the evidence dried all around his face.

"Where have you been, Walter? I was worried that you didn't make it."

"I changed…and it scared me. I didn't have any way of stopping it so I ran and hid under that old bridge over there." Walter explained, pointing over to a collapsed bridge crossing a small creek.

Tears began to stream down Lori's face as she took a piece of her shirt, ripping it off to use as a rag. She scooped up snow into the middle then began to wipe the dried blood from his face and neck. Walter winced a little from the cold but stood his ground as Virginia and the lads shuffled out of the RV and joined them.

Zeus pranced to Walter's side and nudged him over until Walter reached out with a blood stained hand to pet him.

"Wally, is that from the creatures or is it from…..?" Charlie forced himself to ask what he knew everyone, with the exception of Lori, was wondering.

Taking a deep breath and stepping back from everyone. Looking Charlie in the eyes the whole time Walter sighed and replied. "My name is Walter not Wally."

"We know that Walter; don't pay any attention to Charlie right now!"

Focusing on Lori again Walter shrugged his shoulders. "I don't know. I was afraid and running away but I could feel something pulling me over to them. The next thing I know was that I was under that bridge."

"I didn't see him during the fight." Virginia added looking around for back up from the rest.

"I didn't see him." Jermain added.

Charlie shook his head in disbelief. Knowing how Lori felt about Walter and not knowing if he had eaten people or was fighting the creatures was another thing. "Walter, do you know where the herd went?"

Walter snapped his head away from Lori who had begun rubbing the dried blood off again. "No, I don't know; but I can feel them moving away." Reaching his little hand up to Lori's cheek, Walter added, "You can feel them too, right?"

Closing her eyes for the briefest fraction of a moment Lori replied. "Yes, they are moving off to the south."

"How do you know that?" Charlie asked bordering on demanding an answer.

"I don't know Charlie. I just know that they are running a few hours ahead of us... towards someplace south of here."

Standing up and taking Walter by the hand Lori started back towards the RV.

"What are we supposed to do now?" Charlie asked.

"I think we just keep heading towards Clarksville for now. Walter and I will make sure that we ride with the Lads just so everyone can feel safe."

Charlie nodded his head as he headed back to the Suburban. If there was one thing that time with both Lori and Virginia had taught him, it was that they were both stubborn, strong willed women

310

and confronting Lori would only cause the group to break up. Keeping an eye on Walter wouldn't be too hard to do, especially if he was always with the dogs. Everyone knew that nothing could harm Virginia when they were around, not even a zombie Lori or Walter.

The End for now...

A.L. White Books

Z Chronicles: The Beginning

Z Chronicles: Surge of the Dead

Made in the USA
Lexington, KY
27 February 2018